DARK
BROTHER

Book Seven of The Hayle Coven Destinies

PATTI LARSEN

ALSO BY
PATTI LARSEN

The Hayle Coven Universe

The Hunted Series
Fiona Fleming Cozy Mysteries
The Nightshade Cases
The Clone Chronicles
The Diamond City Trilogy
Didi and the Gunslinger

and much, much more.
Find your new favorite author at
pattilarsen.com
Sign up for new releases
bit.ly/pattilarsenemail

ONE

Jean Marc Dumont's trial should have felt like a giant victory. Why then did I sprawl like such a grouch sitting on the hard, stone chair I'd been assigned, glaring around me with my arms crossed over my chest at anyone who even hinted at intruding on my bad mood?

Four days. Four freaking days since my return from the Dark Universe, since my mind and body and soul were torn apart by Creator's sibling, Her heart putting me back together again. Four days since Max's wings were sliced from his drach body, any attempt at regrowth with help from his people and the newly restored Stronghold failing. Four days since a giant chunk of the Universe fell through the crumbling veil and into the void.

And what had I done since returning with a bit of knowledge about the other side and a massive, hulking, metal clad soldier of the Order in tow? Nada. Ziperino.

El Zilcho.

Because now freaking what?

Not a sniff of the other two pieces made it to my son. Gabriel was our only line to the missing chunks of Creator's statue and he'd run up against a blank wall that might as well have been a *hell no* from the Universe itself. Just thinking about the delay made me want to hurt someone. We'd come so far, only to be stymied in the past. Then, in liquid fast time four pieces were located and returned. All within the agenda Fate laid out.

Gabriel told me we were in a race against time at this point. So, if that was true, why were we again sitting on our hands, twiddling our thumbs at each other while the veil fell apart and people vanished into the black nothing?

Because, that's why. Because. And that was the best answer I was getting from anyone who would talk to me. Mom just shrugged, the darkness under her eyes growing deeper by the day. She had her own mess with the NAWC and the fact the other world territories didn't like her plan to make her council all-coven inclusive. They could suck it as far as I was concerned. Piers wasn't much help, the whole renewal of sorcery keeping him busy. He'd been named the leader of the new Sorcerers League and, with Demetrius Strong at his side as his second, he wasn't wasting time taking over the world.

And Jiao's apparent betrayal in the other Universe turned intel gathering mission hadn't given me anything I didn't already know, much to her disappointment. The drachmor jerkfaces would have their punishment, would they ever. They'd pay for what they did to Max, the cowards. Running off like they did to the Dark Universe, abandoning ours. Fate or not, respect wasn't due and I refused to even consider cutting slack. But, it had to hurt Jiao, the fact her turning on me to save me had led her to nothing I didn't uncover myself.

Ack. I really needed a better attitude. At least someone was seeing progress, case in point, as the masses of sorcerers gathered in the room writhed with intense eagerness. And I couldn't think of anyone better to lead them than Piers Southway. Crabbypants I might have been, but I appreciated the fact someone I cared about was in power instead of some asshat who would ruin everything.

He'd been kind enough to offer the distraction of Jean Marc's trial, too. The trip to Scotland wasn't a happy one, though, and part of the reason for my terrible mood. Every time I rode the veil these days I couldn't help but feel its intense pain and sadness, feel the shrinkage of its former limitless potential. There were times it reached out to me like a hurt puppy and asked—not in so many words, mind you—for my help. Explaining to it I was doing my best wasn't going over very well. Try talking to the rubber membrane between the planes sometime in terms it will understand.

Yeah. Crash and burn.

I was big enough to admit my grumpiness was a shield to hide my fear. The frailty and fragility of the constant the veil had been for who knew how many centuries wasn't lost on me. Nor was the fact we were losing whole races and planes into the void, our fault as we rebuilt Creator's statue. And we couldn't stop now, could we? The end of everything was inevitable. Our only hope was to follow this order the new Fate of our Universe, Zoe Helios, and my friend turned-betrayer-turned I didn't know what yet, Trill Zornov, talked about.

Maybe if Trill and Zoe were on the same page. Instead, it seemed like the two were at odds. According to Trill—who I'd recently thought a traitor only to have her guide me to pieces she herself had stolen from me—Zoe was being influenced, that Fate herself was cheating.

Comforting thought. Especially when returning the pieces in order seemed so important. Gabriel stressed it too, even told me some of them had been replaced out of sync. And now I understood placing those pieces linked intrinsically to the very elemental magicks of the Universe. With the right combination of Creator's renewal those powers disappeared into the void as they were supposed to. Was that even something I could accept? They were *supposed to*? How could Creator purposely have set us up to ruin everything?

Questions and more questions and growl, snort,

grumble, grrr.

Whatever reason Zoe had for working for the other side remained a mystery. I couldn't find her, not in the Sanctuary where she'd once lived—where Jean Marc had been captured—nor here in Scotland with the man who loved her, or anywhere else, for that matter. I knew my enemy and the mouthpiece of Dark Brother in this Universe, Liander Belaisle, had his own stronghold somewhere, but the idea she could be working with him just didn't play out. Zoe wouldn't sell us out to Dark Brother. She was Creator's Fate. Whoever was manipulating her, she had to trust them.

I had a few horrible suspicions, but kept them to myself. Because I couldn't find those two, either. But I knew one thing for absolute certain. If Bellanca and Thanos—the original Fates—were involved in this, nothing would save them from me.

A tall, black haired woman collapsed into the stone seat beside me, letting out a loud gust of air. Scowling only made my sister's human form more beautiful, though I wasn't in the mood to tell her so. Meira, the Ruler of Demonicon and the one person in the Universe who wouldn't care if I was crabby to her, tapped her fingernails on the arm rest of her chair and glared back.

"You look happy," she snapped.

"Oh, shut up," I snarled.

Meira grinned suddenly, hands rising to make a nest

of tentacles under her chin. "Tho touchy, Thyd," she said.

The image of her nickname for me flashed in my head, Syd the Squid, actually prodding my funny bone and making me snort.

"How come no one knew you were such a horrible little girl?" I felt myself relax in her presence. I'd always loved my sister, of course I did. But as we got older—as the weight of the Universe settled on us both—it seemed we had only grown closer. With the exception of her fury with me at running away for six months, I think even that had strengthened our bond. I didn't think of her as my baby sis anymore, my Meems. She was Meira, one of my best friends. An equal who understood with more clarity than anyone else in my life just what being me was like.

"Because," she said with a wink of one blue eye, her natural amber showing through her magic for a moment in a flare of demon fire, "they were always so focused on what a jerk you were. Made my job easy."

Fair enough. I reached over and squeezed her hand when it fell back to her armrest. *How are things?*

She shrugged mentally, but her power felt diminished as she let me in, the giant, vast reserve of Demonicon in her possession feeling hollow, echoing. *How do you think?*

I winced and looked away. *I'm sorry, Meems.*

If I thought it was your fault, she sent, *I'd accept that apology.* She sighed in my head. *I should be more afraid, shouldn't I? My entire power base is collapsing, disappearing. The*

Node that holds my planes together burbles happily despite the fact it's falling to pieces while the spirit of our dead grandmother tells me over and over I'm worried about nothing. My people are vanishing into thin air along with their domains. And I'm here at a trial for a former Dumont I really don't give a crap about anymore.

She was right. I realized it as I sat there, inhaling the mildly damp air of the Scottish castle. Where once I'd hated Jean Marc and his family, despised everything they stood for, they didn't seem important any longer. With Andre's death thanks to my werefriend Charlotte's magic curse, the Dumont family power had died with him, leaving his two sons and their former coven to fend for themselves. Whatever became of Kristophe I had no idea. At least he had turned out to be a weak and unthreatening witch who didn't seem all that eager to follow in Daddy's evil footsteps. As for Jean Marc, his possession of the once rare white sorcery had given him an edge over the former Steam Union, gave him leadership of the now defunct Brotherhood. And removed him about as far from my radar as anyone.

I really should have just gone, gotten up and left. Piers could handle this. But even as the thought crossed my mind the main doors to the chamber opened and my tall, blond friend entered, the Dumont eldest in chains behind him.

Trapped. I sagged, shrugged to my sister. *At least this will be quick.*

She sighed and nodded.

Priorities. Funny how much they changed when the Universe was dying.

TWO

So, my sister sent as Piers ascended the dais in the center of the room, Demetrius prodding Jean Marc with power from where he followed. *How are things with your friend over there?*

The complete change of subject startled me, exactly what she'd been aiming for, the brat. If it wasn't for the snarky smirk in her voice I still might not have commented. But her poke triggered my guilt and worry and more than a little attraction to the silent man at my other side. Oliver had saved my life in the Dark Universe—his Universe—ready to throw away his existence to save me. Thanks to a cryptic remark from Zoe I'd saved his butt instead. And despite his worry his presence here meant it would be possible for his people to cross over the barrier dividing our two Universes, my son's assurance he, as the Gateway, would prevent it dispelled that particular fear.

Oh, I had other reservations, naturally. Lots and lots of others to fill in the gaps and leave me shivering in anticipation of what might never come to pass. But at least I didn't have to worry about the Order crashing our party just yet.

Even thinking about Oliver made me turn my head to look at his carved profile. Wide jaw, square and strong with a hint of shadow, cleft chin. High cheekbones, straight nose, deep set but large eyes, heavy brows and a tall forehead leading into dark blond hair. In any other circumstance? Delicious. I was willing to admit it. Not to mention the broad shoulders and chiseled muscles of his tall, strong body from carrying around all that shiny armor. I kind of missed it, to be honest, though he was just as striking in a plaid button up and denims. Big hands with squared off nails that were equal parts rough and soft, warm and firm. And a butt that looked better in jeans than any man's had the right to.

Down girl.

Says you, my demon purred.

You tell her, Shaylee sent with a hint of a blush in her tone. The Sidhe princess soul I carried rarely agreed with my demon side. Just like them to gang up on me now.

We just want you to be happy. My vampire, too? Traitors, the lot of them.

I don't have time for this. I spun back to my sister with

my teeth gritted and addressed her next, though I knew the girls were listening. *As long as he doesn't betray us to Dark Brother, I'm willing to give him the benefit of the doubt.* Guilt instantly smacked me a good one. Oliver had been nothing if not helpful and kind since coming to this Universe. The idea he might betray us seemed utterly ludicrous. Mind you, I'd been known to misread people before. But I just couldn't bring myself to doubt him. He was here for a reason, I'd been driven to bring him here with purpose. If I couldn't trust my own judgment on the fact, I could at least hang my hat on that.

I just hoped he hadn't overheard my doubt. From what I could tell, he was doing a good enough job worrying about his presence here for the both of us.

My sister's eyes narrowed, her lips lifting, teeth showing. Clearly, she wasn't done with me or the subject of Oliver just yet.

And a place to crash at your house. The lewd connotation wasn't lost on me as my sister grinned. She leaned forward, wiggling her fingers at Oliver. He smiled back, white teeth showing, before waving in return.

You know how to kidnap them. I almost laughed out loud at her suggestive comment.

Considering your husband, I grinned openly now, happy to have something to rub in myself, *took me hostage when we first met, you might want to rethink the teasing, sister.*

She tossed her head, glossy curls bouncing.

Rameranselot might have chosen you as a target, she said, all arrogance, *but he married* me. *Chew on that, Thquid.*

Double snort. *Thanks*, I sent in a tighter, softer touch as Piers's British accented voice began to fill the space, the attention of everyone in the room focused on him and the accusations he leveled against Jean Marc. I was already intimately aware of the details of his arrest so I didn't care to listen. *I needed the laugh.*

Me, too. Meira's fingers closed over mine, jaw jumping. She'd taken up pacing as a means of concentration, my favorite, too. Guess teeth grinding ran in the family as well. *Tell me we're going to be okay.*

I didn't comment. Because I refused to lie to her. I just didn't know for sure. Not because of anything on Creator's part, or Fate's for that matter, despite me wishing I could pass the buck. Too much was simply still unanswered for me to even guess as to the end result. And my own role, whatever it might end up being, was tied to the name Doombringer. So there remained the deep and crushing fear I'd be the ruin of everything.

As Piers's voice droned on, the list of charges against Jean Marc growing by the moment, I forced myself to focus on meditation breathing just to keep from jiggling my knees in agitation. It didn't help, not really, but saved me from looking like an anxious preteen at her first dance.

The collection of sorcerers who observed didn't seem

to have my attention deficit issues. Their anger and frustration completely pinned Jean Marc to the dais without needing power to do it. How must it have felt to have all that animosity pushing down on his shoulders? I'd been in his position a time or two, so I guess I knew, didn't I?

Better him than me.

Oliver's hand lifted, ran over the side of his jaw with a scratching sound, the faint beard on his face rasping against his knuckles. I caught myself staring at him again and had to force my eyes forward while my demon chuckled and muttered something that made Shaylee gasp.

It didn't help I found myself growing attached to the Order soldier sitting so quietly and patiently beside me. And, if I was going to be completely honest with myself, I liked knowing he was always there. Never judging, not interfering. Just a looming, blond shadow that seemed focused on one thing and one thing only: yours truly. That kind of attention can be heady for a girl. And it's not like he was leering or gross about it. Not in the least. Maybe if he was I could have shaken these feelings trying to worm their way into my heart. Oliver's calm, kind and intense attention was, instead, respectful and even hopeful.

Why couldn't he have just been a jerk? I had thought he might be. I judged him that way when we first met that day in my cell on the other side of the barrier between Universes. He'd come across as arrogant, amused by my predicament instead of treating my capture and assault by Dark Brother with the weight I thought it deserved. Still, it didn't take me long to realize he saw everything around him with a hint of good humor, even the darkest moments colored by his delightfully soft optimism. Shocking, honestly, the last thing I expected from a solider of the Order. I'd lived in fear of that army for a long time now, since my son's power opened a pathway that almost allowed them to march into my Universe. The sheer destructive force of them came across loud and clear. Or, I'd thought so. Oliver, on the other hand, was the complete opposite of what I'd come to fear. Instead of being forced to dive into irritation to hide my anxiety, my usual go-to, I grew to like his sense of humor the last four days, to appreciate his opinion and to listen when he spoke, even though speaking up was rare for him.

To think of him as a person, not a soldier of my enemy and the greatest threat my Universe had ever faced.

That did nothing to help the truth, though. I couldn't let him in. My own jaw tightened as I sank further into the uncomfortable seat with a perfect view of the last few minutes of Jean Marc's life and told myself in no uncertain terms any possible hope of having a relationship with anyone, let alone an enemy of my entire

Universe, was out of the freaking question.

Spoil sport, my demon grumbled.

You're not even giving him a chance. Shaylee sulked, mentally prodding me. *You know you're attracted to him.*

So what? I shot it back at them, grim, angry. *Yes, I admit it. He's hot, I'd love to know what his lips taste like—* demon chuckled—*and he's either going to rejoin his people and try to kill us all or vanish when his Universe goes kablooey.*

That shut them up.

Or, my vampire sent, her usual calm the voice of reason, *he's exactly what you need right now.*

Not you, too. I tossed that at her, sullen complaint making me feel small again. *I thought you at least would see reason.*

She sighed, shrugged. *There are times, Syd, when we must grasp for whatever warmth we can find, whatever shelter in an oncoming storm. And to hell with what comes after.*

Because we don't know if there will be an after, Shaylee whispered.

Amen, my demon sent.

I purposely shut them out, with nothing to say to contradict them. Maybe they were right. But this was neither the time nor the place to contemplate what to do about Oliver.

"How does the accused plead to the charges?" Piers turned to face Jean Marc.

Finally, the good part. My demon's grin was back.

Savage. Shaylee sniffed.

You were the one who suggested burying him alive, demon sent.

Children, my vampire murmured. *Pay attention.*

Good humor back, I focused on Jean Marc and the snarl on his face as he spit at Piers's feet.

"I'd do it all again," he growled. "Only I'd find a way to kill you."

At least he was honest.

Piers just smiled, smearing the gleam of saliva on the stone floor with the toe of his Italian leather shoe. "For your crimes, Jean Marc Dumont, I sentence you to death."

No one looked surprised. That is, not at the sentence. But when a black tunnel opened, a shout of shock coming from the guards who protected the space telling me they weren't expecting company, I think surprise was the least of our reactions.

Especially when, smiling like a cat who ate something delicious and precious to me, Liander Belaisle sauntered through with Eva Southway right beside him. Before anyone could react, attack, do anything, Belaisle's voice rang in the air.

"You call this a trial?" He spun around, glaring with his light yellow eyes, teeth flashing a cunning smile.

"Arrest them both." Piers's own voice shook, his power snaking out, aided by the white sorcery at his command, slamming into a wall of magic to be dispersed in a puff of smoke.

"Nice try," Belaisle said, bowing from the waist in a mocking salute. "Now, if you don't mind, I'd like a moment with my client."

Piers sputtered, the entire room silent in surprise, even me. Such audacity couldn't be comprehended. It just couldn't. Exactly what I'd expect from Belaisle. Why was I really surprised to find him here, smiling directly at me, daring me to come for him? At least Eva had the good sense to look uncomfortable and shifty about her presence as my friend finally managed to speak.

"Your what?" Piers's normally polished tone was harsh with shock.

"That's right," Belaisle said, bright and shining. "As his legal representation, I'm here to defend Jean Marc against all comers."

THREE

If it wasn't so laughably ridiculous I'd have been lunging physically over the heads of those sitting in front of me and launching myself at Belaisle to tear that smirk from his face. Instead, I shook my head, prodding his power with mine, feeling Dark Brother's influence and wondering for the first time what would happen, really happen, if he and I were in a position to fight right here and now.

The prospect appealed.

Instead, Eva Southway stepped past him, staring down her son with her crazy showing. She'd let her close cropped blonde hair grow out into a shaggy bob in desperate need of a haircut, her normally thin face now gaunt and lined. She'd aged from the handsome woman I'd first met, become hard and world weary, through fault of her own and through loss. Grief I understood. It had driven me to lengths and tasks I'd never thought myself capable. But hers took her the other direction entirely. Away from family, though it was the loss of her brother to the enemy that drove her over the edge according to Piers. Whatever possessed her to join forces with the very man who was the death of her beloved sibling was beyond me, though I never put anything past Eva. For all I knew she had a knife prepared for the center of Belaisle's back. And though I wouldn't miss him and would likely thank her for saving me the effort of killing him personally, I doubted such a plan would succeed. Not with Dark Brother as his mascot.

And while Eva had abandoned the Steam Union, betrayed her own son, all of them by joining forces with Belaisle, I felt the old loyalty in the room, the sway of her presence. The bulk of the men and women who'd come to the castle for the trial were former Steam Union sorcerers. They'd followed Eva for a long time, through darkness and death. And despite her past they were inclined to listen.

So was I. If only to find out what she was up to.

"My people." Way to play the commonality card. No one seemed disinclined to silence her, not even her scowling son who stared at his mother as if he would personally rip her heart out and feed it to her. Her voice had lost none of its power, at least, her tone none of its command. "Every sorcerer deserves the right to a fair trial. Especially now."

Now that the Universe was falling apart, she meant? Or now that the power ties had been cut and it was every sorcerer for himself?

Piers spoke up, ignoring Belaisle in favor of his mother. That was okay. I wasn't going to let the smarmy former Brotherhood leader out of my sight or my magic for that matter. I slid white sorcery under the lip of the shielding surrounding Belaisle and Eva, flexing slightly to test the waters. "Jean Marc Dumont," Piers said in a gruff and furious voice, "is guilty of all charges and has denied nothing. In fact," he took a half step toward his mother before visibly taking control of his temper, "he's confessed to many of them."

"Without proper counsel," Belaisle said, slick as slime. I couldn't help but picture black ooze coating his tongue despite his expensive, pinstriped suit, his fresh haircut, the razor sharp lines of his precise goatee. Somehow, all that perfection just made his arguments all the more revolting. "All such confessions should be thrown out and this mockery of justice overturned." I hated the reasonable tone in his voice, the way his hands spread before him in supplication, gold rings catching the light. I had to admit, despite his short stature, Belaisle always carried himself like a leader, like a ruler. Confidence had never been one of his issues, at least as far as I could tell. It was trusting him about as far as I could toss his designer suited body that was the problem. "Haven't we lost enough of our people over the years? Isn't it time to end our differences as a race and look to empathy and compassion for those misguided by the way things used to be?"

They were listening, weren't they? How familiar this seemed, like a vinyl record skipping back over and over the same, sad argument. I'd heard it from witches for years. And now, from his smarmy mouth. It was just too damned much.

I laughed out loud in the quiet that followed his pretty little speech. I know I should have stayed out of it but I just couldn't stop the sound. I'd like to blame my demon for the outburst, but frankly we were all guilty.

Eyes turned to me, some with regret, some with anger, a few with their own guilt showing. Too late to backpedal, I stood and slid down the row, doing my best to not look like a fumbling idiot tripping over people's feet. Fortunately, whether out of concern for their safety or respect for who I was, I was granted an easy exit and, at last, descended with slow and deliberate steps to the dais in the center of the room.

The focus of attention? Yeah, been here before. My turn to carry the weight of all those eyes.

Piers glared, though I knew his anger wasn't aimed at me. *Sorry*, I sent, all he was getting at the moment, before turning to Belaisle. How civilized our little meeting, enforced by a barrier fed by Creator's sibling. My magic flexed again, pushing that barrier, met resistance as gigantic as Dark Brother. It took a massive amount of self-control not to flinch from it, from the memory of what He did to me in His Universe. Of the week lost to the explorations of the massive mind and power that controlled the other side. Pretty proud of myself as I instead latched onto the edges of it and sent a direct message to Belaisle.

Whatever your game is, a trickle of white sorcery tested the boundary once again, *we're not buying it, Liander.*

Maybe not you, he sent back, the echoing darkness of his master in his mind, *but they are.*

I could feel he was right and immediately suspected tampering. Why hadn't I before? Too distracted by the whole show, just as Belaisle wanted. I hated he'd played me yet again, answered his taunt with a wash of white sorcery. It tore through the room, cleared up that mess. *Thanks for the reminder*, I sent with a smile. And wondered how much of Liander actually survived in there. He'd never have made that kind of mistake on his own. Arrogant he might have been, but stupid?

He snarled as the tone of the space changed instantly, sorcerers shaking their heads. Even Piers and Demetrius looked startled, but no more than I was when I felt a familiar looming shape beside me and the pressure of power not of our Universe. Part of me wished he'd stayed the hell out of it, but I couldn't blame the Order soldier at my side for making himself known.

It was the huge, staring gaze of Belaisle that brought me the most satisfaction as he gaped upward at Oliver. But not due to anything I'd done, oh no. The utter shock on his face, the disbelief, ran deep and shuddering through Belaisle as Dark Brother Himself processed what He was seeing.

The fact He didn't know He'd lost one of His people into our Universe made me pause and wonder yet again while Belaisle spluttered and Eva shrank back, no longer sure of herself.

"Impossible." Dark Brother spoke through Belaisle's lips much like I'd heard Creator speak through Zoe. Either His people had kept the truth from Him or they thought Oliver dead. There had been enough of the drachmor—the evolved drach gone to the Dark Universe—and Order soldiers in Max's prison pit when we'd fled through the Gateway for home they must have realized I took Oliver with me.

Or not. My vampire's soft voice broke through. *Perhaps they thought him dead after all, that you'd killed him. Or that he didn't survive the passage.*

Because he shouldn't be here. Shaylee sighed as understanding passed over Belaisle's face. I should have been worried, right? Maybe keeping Oliver from showing his face was the smarter choice after all. Too late. Dark Brother now knew for certain one of His people was here in my Universe. Oliver warned me when he first arrived this meant the Order could find him and follow him over, ruining everything. But they hadn't yet. Maybe because they hadn't realized he was here.

Damn it. Did we just give them reason to try? Still, the stuttering slowness that was Dark Brother's process actually brought me comfort. Uber powerful He might be. But old school and slow to process and act? I'd take that as a weapon.

I feel the power of my Universe in them. Oliver's warning came as he spoke out loud. Like I didn't know Belaisle and Eva had been tampered with. Snarl. "You'd be surprised what is possible here, Master."

Not talking to Belaisle, clearly. *You think sarcasm is smart?*

Oliver's mind shivered with nervous laughter, light and anxious and childlike in his defiant glee. Like he'd been waiting for this moment his whole life and, despite terror, was enjoying himself immensely. *I take it you have a better idea.*

Now that he mentioned it. I hit the barrier before me with white sorcery, feeling Piers and Demetrius join me. My sister landed hard on the dais in her full demon form, amber eyes on fire, adding her magic. Oddly, Oliver held back while the four of us pummeled Belaisle's shielding and Dark Brother stared at us through his pale, yellow gaze.

"The new power." He sounded dull, controlled. I knew the feeling of Dark Brother well enough to shudder from that voice but held my ground anyway. Go me. "You will bring it to me, soldier."

Oliver swayed, face paling, and for the first time I truly worried he might betray us after all. I'd been in his place, under the pressure that was the massive magic of the other Universe's master. Knew beyond a doubt such a demand was impossible to resist, that we were lost and Oliver, through no fault of his own, was about to destroy us all.

And then, to my utter shock and delight—and more than a little angry envy at his strength—Oliver shook his head as I reached for him with magic. He blocked me, shoulders back, expression settling into grim determination. I brushed the edge of the pressure forcing itself on him and understood. Creator's sibling only had a portion of His magic here, at best the most Belaisle could muster as His channel in this Universe. Augmented, yes. But not the all-consuming and devouring power I'd faced. Shame on me for the hint of satisfaction at that fact, that Oliver wasn't stronger than me after all. Followed by relief. While Oliver might not have been feeling the full weight of Dark Brother's presence, I finally winced in sympathy at how much effort it had to have taken him to remain upright and defiant. "I will not."

Dark Brother roared through Belaisle's mouth, a wash

of power escaping the shielding. But instead of attacking us I felt the presence flee, retreating and leaving the now desperate Eva and Belaisle to fumble for enough strength to hold us off.

This is the real reason they want Jean Marc, my demon sent.

Dark Brother finally sat up and took notice of the white sorcery. Shaylee's agreement came with a rumble of anger.

Agreed, my vampire sent. *Shall we deny him that prize?*

I felt their escape coming, grinned at Belaisle as my now superior magic encased him in a net of glowing white that cascaded rainbow sparks. And yet, still, I should have known better, understood there was more at work here than just my need to crush these two and never have them trouble me again.

The moment Trill appeared, her sad face downcast, dark eyes full of despair, I accepted despite myself. And didn't fight her when she cut off our attack with magic of her own. Nor did I complain when, with a dark scowl and a harsh hand, Belaisle lunged and grasped Jean Marc in his grip, jerking the cowed Dumont into a black tunnel, Eva escaping behind him.

Oh, I wanted to. About as much as I wished I could grasp Trill Zornov's shoulders in my hands and shake her until she told me what the hell was really going on. But I didn't. I made a choice, the same one I'd decided on when She saved me, Her heart healing me in Dark

Brother's prison. To trust Fate and Creator like I'd never done before and watch in silent frustration as Trill disappeared.

FOUR

The room erupted into angry chaos, people yelling at each other, at Piers, at me. I ignored all of them, teeth aching while I fought against my ingrained need to do something. To fix things and be the action hero. Instead, I just let them go.

Maybe I was growing up or losing my mind or had just cracked completely.

Thank you for trusting me. Trill's distant whisper made me sigh and unclench.

You're welcome.

Damn it.

Piers's people cleared the room while he barked orders before spinning on me, my giant, red skinned sister looming on one side, Oliver's not inconsiderable bulk on the other. Like I needed bodyguards. Still, it was nice to have them on my team when my furious friend finally got around to chewing me out.

"What the actual hell." Pier's hair quivered he was shaking so hard, the spill of silky blond to his knees rippling with the motion. "Syd." He swallowed hard while Demetrius shook his head at me, sympathy on his face. At least he didn't hate me. "I take it there's an excellent reason my mother and Belaisle and Jean Marc Bloody Dumont," his voice rose and fell with feeling and temper, British accent sharp in his rage, "aren't dead right now." He stabbed one finger at the ground beneath him, a crack appearing in the stone with a loud bang. "At my feet."

I shrugged, not exactly deciding on casual as much as using it as a default. "Trusting the Universe over here," I said.

At first I worried my choice of attitude had just alienated him all over again, like I did when I left to join the drach. I couldn't bear the thought my old friend hated me, blamed me. When his gray eyes tightened around the sides, the deep, dark circles under them pulsing with tiny veins, his long fingered hands clenching into fists so tight his pale skin went translucent, I worried.

And then, like a balloon losing air from a gaping wound, Piers exhaled and sagged, head falling forward, shoulders rounding down, hands unwinding. Pain and despair colored his gaze as he shrugged, helpless.

I know, I sent, hopefully with enough compassion and

kindness he understood I really did. *Piers. We're so screwed. But we have to believe in something. And I'm tired of fighting Creator when she's going to make us do what she wants regardless.*

He bobbed a nod, wiped at his mouth with the back of one hand. *I should know better than to argue or even try to win,* he sent. *With a love like Zoe.* His girlfriend was Fate, right. Poor sucker. His gaze drifted off out a window into the dark, Scottish evening. When he turned back to me again, he managed a smile.

"Do I know how to throw a party," he said, "or what?"

I laughed, hugged him impulsively, feeling how thin he'd become under his longcoat and button up, how a shiver of shock still ran through him. He felt different, too, without the linkage to the Steam Union and full now of Creator's ultimate magic. I missed our tie to each other, having to fend off the black line of sorcery wanting to bind us all over again. But, the white magic shunted it aside for me before I could act. That, at least, we could keep. And his mother couldn't track, the whole reason we were forced to maintain our magical distance.

Until she and Belaisle got their hands on some white sorcery, that was. Ah. Yeah. Just happened, didn't it?

"Curious." Oliver's deep voice startled me, startled all of us. He so rarely spoke in public, preferring, it seemed to me, to observe, though he never had a problem talking to me when we were alone. My sister shifted back to human form even as she nodded.

"I think we're on the same idea," she said. "The white sorcery."

Oliver's brow pinched, but out of curiosity and consideration more than concern. "Why, now that it's so prolific and widespread, have those two not managed to steal some yet?"

Why didn't I think of that? "Dark Brother?"

Oliver's lips turned down at the corners and he nodded slowly, but still seemed to be working things out. "Possibly," he said. And looked up, gray eyes glinting green as they met mine. "Yes, you may have hit on it, Syd. If He's controlling them as much as my people are accustomed to, the Master wouldn't allow the white sorcery in."

"But now that He knows about it," I said, "and wants it..."

Oliver sighed, shook his head, overgrown blond hair brushing his cheeks. "They have access now. And while it may take Him some time to assimilate it, it will happen." He flinched as if guilty of something, smiling now, if softly. "To think I could speak so openly against Him," he said, "and not be reprimanded."

"Speak away," Meira said at her most dry. "Chase down the idea, Oliver. We're listening."

He nodded, ran one hand over his mouth as he did, staring at the crack Piers had made in the floor as if to help him concentrate. I hoped the parallel to the destruction of the Universe wasn't some kind of omen. "We've had no real change in anything in our Universe for as long as we've had history." He paced two steps then back again. Nice to know we shared that little habit. When he stopped at my side, his shoulder brushed mine and I welcomed the contact. "I've been observing all of you carefully. Not as a spy." He dropped his hand, eyes wide as he looked around at all of us. I smiled in reassurance and gestured for him to go on. "But out of wonder," he said. "You've all evolved, haven't you? And even these powers you control, they feel... like growing things." He shook his head again, tossed his hands as if giving up on old notions. "I've never felt that of my own power. We have, as a race, had a certain strength since our conception and that strength has never changed. The only exception to that rule has been the drachmor. But even they have remained static for the centuries they have been in my Universe."

Interesting. "As if Dark Brother gave you everything He wanted to give you from day one and then that was it?"

Oliver nodded to me, a faint hint of relief in his eyes. "Yes, I think you nailed it, Syd. And perhaps is now unable to change that."

"Whereas Creator's path was different." Meira was nodding, too, amber showing in her eyes.

"Makes sense," I said. "The fractured magicks might have had something to do with that. So how can we use this to our advantage?"

"I don't know that we can," Oliver said, sounding suddenly chastised, backing up a half step. "Sorry to waste time talking about it. The truth doesn't make my people any less powerful. And despite His reticence for change, now that my Master," he swallowed, "Dark Brother has white sorcery, He will find a way to use it for His own purposes."

I reached out, grasped his elbow, pulled him forward so he was in our circle again. "It might be hugely helpful," I said, "or it might be trivia for later. Regardless, we don't judge and we don't ignore any chance to work things out."

Oliver's smile returned, faint and thankful. "I just wish I could be of more help." Another frown, this time with a glimmer of the humor I'd seen in him the first time we'd met. It had to be hard for him, knowing the others didn't trust him completely, being an enemy solider trying to prove himself. If he was, in fact, on our side. I shook that off while Oliver spoke. "You know, there's one option that might piss Him off and shake Him up."

"We're open to that." Piers grinned and, in that instant, I saw him visibly accept Oliver even as Demetrius's cherub face warmed into a smile, too. Two down, a bunch to go. But I'd take it.

We count too, you know, my demon sent.

And so do I. Meira's mind met mine. *For better or worse, he's here and we have to take advantage of that. Trust, well, that's just a concept.*

"Let's hear it," I said.

"Give white sorcery to everyone." Oliver shrugged, grinning openly.

We'd been spreading it among our allies already, but everyone? "You mean normals too?"

"Everyone." He met our eyes evenly, calmly, so reasonable. "Spread it far and wide until the whole Universe is full of it."

What was left of the Universe. "You think that will counter Dark Brother?"

Oliver's smile faded and he shrugged. "He won't understand it," he said, quiet and internalizing something that hurt, clearly. "And it might slow Him down, confuse Him. It won't stop Him, ultimately. But it could buy us some time."

So, no real strategic advantage, but at least the playing field would be back to even. But how much would such an act change our Universe? Then again, wasn't that Creator's plan all along?

"I like it." Meira clapped Oliver on the shoulder and grinned. "Worst case scenario we all go out in a blaze of glory."

I'd have loved to counter the delightful mental image

her statement raised in my head, but interruptions had a habit of happening to me. And this one caught my attention immediately.

Syd, Charlotte sent, my werefriend and queen of the werenation feeling more than a little wolfish as she touched my mind. *You need to come. Now.*

No matter how powerful I became or who Creator intended me to be, somehow Charlotte could always make me come running.

On my way. Because I had to at least pretend she didn't just order me around.

FIVE

Meira left us then, promising to give white sorcery to every demon still left under her rule. The more I thought about it, the more sense it made. Why were we hoarding the new magic, anyway? Well, not hoarding exactly, but I'd been kind of keeping it to my own inner circle. Oliver's suggestion made me shake my head at myself. White sorcery was Creator's intent for magic in our Universe. Time to do as She wished and put it out there for all to utilize.

Of course, as we left Scotland and headed toward Charlotte and Danilo waiting for us in Ukraine, I wondered if doing so might trigger bigger changes than we expected. I already knew every person on our plane had access to sorcery. While it had been a bit of a shock at first, the fact of the matter was it made sense.

Everything was ruled by sorcery, from the smallest molecule to the giant drach. As for normals, some woke to use it and others didn't. I still didn't understand that particular why and might never at this point, considering white sorcery was the wave of the future. If we had a future.

Regardless the ultimate fate of the Universe, the vast majority of the human normals on this world remained in the dark, so to speak. Would opening white sorcery to the entirety of creation change that? While I'd often wondered what it would be like to live in a civilization unafraid of magic, the consequences initially could be devastating. The Brotherhood's grand plan to terrorize and control witchdom had seen to that. Modern culture saw magic as either impossible or evil. Or a sham designed to bilk innocent gullibles out of their money. The very idea of exposing normals to the truth had an equal mix of appeal and horror. Yes, living openly had its interesting aspects. But the mass destruction and mayhem such a reveal would stir would have to be very carefully contained and controlled.

Look at me, planning out the future of a plane I was on a path to destroy along with the rest of the Universe. Couldn't help myself as I passed out of the damp afternoon chill in Scotland to the cool crispness of evening in Ukraine. At least if such a thing happened, if normals were to come to realize magic was real and they were surrounded by paranormals... at least they would have a highly trained backup to take them in hand and show them how to handle their new power.

I just couldn't think about such a thing right now. Worrying about what might happen would lead me down roads that would distract from what mattered. As usual, if disaster struck, I'd be here, ready and waiting, to handle it.

Why did the thought of that depress me so much?

Charlotte had given me permission to enter the werepalace from the veil long ago, but it still felt a bit like walking into someone's private quarters without knocking. I'd grown so accustomed to touching down on the grassy lawn outside the sprawling building complex it felt odd to just step out into the sitting room attached to her suite. She didn't react adversely to my entrance, as calm and collected as ever, though Danilo scowled faintly at my appearance. Like the former wereking had even an iota of say into the protocols his sister enacted. He'd betrayed his entire race to the Russian mafia for the sake of revenge. He could bite me.

They weren't alone, aside from the two wereguards at the door. Charlotte's mate and Prince Consort, Sage America, nodded to me from where he stood, arms crossed over his chest, glaring at the visitor who trembled ever so slightly in the chair across from Charlotte. The small mafia man's rotundness had returned, cheeks pale and a faint sheen of sweat standing out on his brow. Iosif

Grechnev looked nervous. Not that I blamed him. He knew exactly who I was, who Charlotte and her werepeople were, and the truth of it had to terrify his normal soul.

His beady, dark eyes took in Oliver with a sweep before he stood, swallowing hard, and offered one pudgy hand to me. Gone was the false appearance he'd taken on in Las Vegas where Sass, Charlotte and I tracked him down. His attempt to escape the mafia led to a disguise that ill-suited him. He looked much as he had in the restaurant here in Ukraine where we'd first met and smelled strongly of cheap cigars and borsht.

I stepped forward and, to his surprise, took his offered hand, shook it. And froze at what I felt.

Had it happened so soon, perhaps stirred by what I'd been thinking just moments before arriving here? Or on its own, perhaps? The very thing I'd considered, the worry sharing white sorcery would waken power in normals… but no. The dark, hungry feeling inside him had nothing to do with that new, ultimate magic. But there was no denying the truth, not with his damp skin pressed to mine, thin trails of black oozing upward to sniff at the blossom of darkness at my feet.

"Someone has woken your sorcery." Not a question for him. And the reason, I now understood, for his nervousness. Iosif nodded quickly, his power weak but steady, shaking a bit around the edges, a newborn fawn trembling on narrow legs but curious about the world around it. "Who?"

He retrieved his hand with a quick jerk and only then did I realize I'd been clinging to him with some force. "My bosses," he said with a simple shrug like that should explain everything. It didn't and the grinding of my teeth must have told him as much. He glanced at Charlotte with real worry on his face before looking back to me, hands in the air as though to ward off an attack pending. His power rose in answer, though I knew the defense attempt was automatic, felt his sorcery react to his fear. His bosses had so much to answer for and this just added to that list. Sending out an untrained, newly woken sorcerer into the world was a recipe for crash, burn, boom. "As a reward," he said, unaware of the fact I was building shielding around his seeking power, doing what I could to keep him from going feral. Without support or any kind of guidance, his sorcery would overtake his will. I knew that, they should know that if they had the ability to wake him. What the hell were they doing? "I found a way to explain my absence." His defection, he meant. One of those thick hands ran across his almost bald head, shaking and wary, a tell gesture, perhaps. I filed it then ignored it, my wards finally sealing up around him and containing the pulsing hunger of his sorcery. Sure, it was thin and weak now, but give it a bit. I was surprised it hadn't begun randomly feeding yet. Must have happened within the last day or so. I exhaled and shot a look at Charlotte. Her steady, level gaze told me she knew what I'd just done and approved. "I've been appointed the new leader of Nickolay Vetrov's territory and granted power of my own." That caught my attention at last. He sounded faintly prideful despite his anxiety but I let him have it.

"I see." I left that hanging, menacing without speaking further. Watched the distant puffed up feeling he had for what he'd accomplished fall away while his mind twisted around visibly behind his eyes. Was I really so terrifying? No matter. The fact he'd replaced that cruel and disgusting monster was either a good thing for us or a very bad thing for Iosif.

"They've told me all about you," he said, stumbling through the words with his accent thicker than usual. So, depending on the holes in his knowledge they'd filled in, and how much they actually understood, he was right now debating crapping his pants in favor of running. Awesome. "More than I ever knew before." He swallowed again, steadied himself. "Doombringer."

That hurt, more than he would ever know, and my entire body reacted to the name. I snarled without meaning to, losing my temper over the sound of those words strung together. When had I come to hate the title I bore? And why did it feel like this newbie piece of crap didn't have the right to use it?

Iosif backpedaled a half step, swaying, face graying out as he gulped a breath of air in response, hands held out again. "I have news." Like that would save him.

"Better be good." I turned away at last, entire body tense. That his bosses knew about my Doombringer status made me immensely upset, fired up my demon, Shaylee's irritation, even my vampire's cold rage. How much had they uncovered? Was Belaisle to blame, Eva? So much I didn't know. The fact, however, they were able to wake sorcery in Iosif told me more than his words.

They still had Black Soul sorcerers among them.

SIX

"Why you?" Biting, that question, full of command and demanding more than maybe he was able to give.

Iosif shivered, shrugged. "Why not me?"

I snapped my teeth together so hard my head rang. "They didn't grant that power to your predecessor." I knew that much, at least. Intimately. I'd killed Nicolay with my magic, stopped his evil heart personally. Felt no power in him, only that of Konstantin present at that time. So, why suddenly were they waking their lieutenants? What changed?

We're not going to like it, my vampire sighed.

Iosif glanced at Charlotte then back to me, voice dropping low. "I don't know," he said. "But there are more of us. Many more." Not so special then, was he?

Oh, Syd. Suck it up and focus.

"Fine," I said. "Tell me why you're here. Why I'm

here." Better be good. My temper was rising by the second at the thought of the mafia and their pet sorcerers making mockery of the power I'd fought so hard for. Given up so much to protect and nourish. As that thought build, I shook slightly, forced to ram my fists into my pockets to keep from shaking him.

Iosif must have sensed or seen my growing anger, because he sank into his chair again with a fearful sigh, the fabric hissing against his expensive suit. "I know what has been done to Femke Svennson," he said, sounding sad despite his nervousness. "You're not going to like it."

Had to be hard for him to admit. I'd give him that. "I already know," I said, refusing to give him anything at all to take my edge off. Let him know he was useless to me, worthless. Let him quiver in terror he had nothing, was nothing.

Jeeze, Syd. Grip. As in get a.

"When I returned to my bosses, they believed the story Sharlotta and I conceived." Iosif hurried on. "That I had been spying on the werewolves on the West coast. I even shared information about the fallen Brotherhood through the Hensley coven." Those words stumbled from him as I spun and glared, angry with Charlotte for using one of my darkest acts for our purposes but understanding why she did it. "They accepted me into their inner circle at last." There was the pride again. Snarl. And yet, why not? Surely this was something he'd longed for since joining the mafia. Had no idea I was considering taking all of that away with a crushing blow to his new power. I could seal him up right here and now, forever. And nothing would open him again. "You understand she's been infected with a fraction of the soul of the fallen sorcerer, Konstantin?"

I nodded, held it together long enough to answer. "So I discovered."

He wrung his hands together before grasping the arms of the chair firmly, the scent of his sweat finally reaching me in the heavy air. I held my breath, the faint sounds of the werewolves on the other side of the door carrying out their tasks and lives distant, like a dream, the crackle of the fire beside Sage counterpoint. Details. Focus on the present, the moment. My anger began to ease as I breathed into the instant. "The affliction," he said, dread in his tone, "is irreversible."

Knee jerk made me snarl even as I hit him with power. Not hard, just enough. I needed that, to express my instant unhappiness in some tangible way. To make him suffer for that lie.

I refused to believe him. My entire being rejected his words as I strode forward and stood before him, knowing the girls showed their power in their own anger, feeling amber fire crackle, the rumble of the ground beneath the werepalace, how white sparks appeared in the corners of my vision. Hated suddenly being a bully, knowing that was exactly the road I galloped down. Iosif shrank from me, though his sorcery bubbled upward against my shields in an attempt to protect him. My own blossom of darkness leaped into full wakefulness and butted against the edge of his in warning.

"Why?"

He glanced around as though desperate for something to tell me. "I don't know," he finally admitted. "It's what they told me, I swear."

"You don't know much, Iosif," I said, quiet, threatening. "Makes me wonder how useful you really are to me."

Charlotte chuffed softly in my head as the small mafia man pushed himself physically back into his chair.

While I understand your anger, she sent in that cool, precise way she had, I'd rather keep him intact a little while longer.

Suit yourself, I shot at her. But the next time you summon me to talk to this pathetic little worm, make sure he has information I can use.

Charlotte flinched from me, just a fraction. Enough I knew I'd gone too far with her.

Yes, Doombringer, she sent.

Oh no she did not. Sorry, I sent back, grudging but truly apologetic.

We're all trying, Syd, she sent.

Temper dampened by our exchange, I shook my

head, bent over Iosif, hands on the back of his chair, face inches from his. "Maybe saving Femke is impossible for your bosses," I said. "But they aren't me."

He nodded, gulped. "Of course," he said. "I'm sure there is a way."

Liar. And that, sadly, was the worst of the matter. I wished he'd continued to argue instead of leaving me with the terrible fear there really was no cure.

"Tell me how many survived." I turned away from him again. "The Black Souls, Iosif. How many."

He choked a moment and, as I spun again, the redness of his face, the way he squirmed in his seat, told me I wasn't going to like what he had to say, even less than the news about Femke.

"Don't kill me," he whispered, hoarse and tense. "It's not my fault." He glanced at Charlotte who shrugged and looked away. So much for her needing him. She appeared unwilling to defend him further. It was then all the anger poured out of me and left me limp. Poor Iosif, I really did feel sorry for him in that moment. He'd come to help, for whatever reason. Sure, it might have been fear driving him, fear of me, of Charlotte. Or maybe there was more to him than I was willing to accept.

Such a switch of emotion, enough I was getting a headache from it. He seemed so small just then, so fragile. And, if I had to admit it, brave. I'd give him that much. Still, I had to know.

"Just spit it out," I said.

He finally pulled himself under control and exhaled before grunting something in Russian.

"I didn't hear you."

He nodded. "Doombringer," he said. That name again. Didn't illicit the same response as the first time. Good for me. "You want to know how many survived? Better to ask how they disappeared."

Oh. My. Swearword. "They didn't die off, did they? How many escaped?"

He sagged in the chair, all the wind knocked out of him as he spoke again. "All of them."

SEVEN

I had to sit down. And did, this time the one who sagged and sighed, feeling my entire body release all tension in an effort to not feel utterly defeated. I'd thought this battle fought and won long ago, a handful of the terrible sorcerer sect killed and left for dust. Only to find out now, so late in the game, they hadn't been eradicated after all.

"Tell me," I said, unhappy with the weariness in my voice. Like I needed more things to worry about.

He nodded abruptly, an eager puppy wanting to please me. Whether my change in attitude freed his tongue and stress or he simply needed to get it all out, Iosif leaned forward and focused his words and attention on me in a rush of English broken occasionally by his native tongue.

"I now believe all of my bosses, all of the leaders of

the *русская мафия*, to be what you call Black Souls." He shuddered, one hand running over his mouth, rasping across his mustache. "We call them *chernaya dusha*." Sounded worse in Russian. "They took over many years ago, from what I have been able to uncover, decades. Once only a handful of those who weren't with power knew of their existence and rule. But that's changing quickly. And once one of us is instated, our power woken, we are tied to our masters forever." He shivered at that, hands balling in his lap.

I felt his sorcery, the ties that bound. Not like the old ones, the bonds of awakening that used to rule sorcery before Gabriel returned Creator's missing arm. No, this was different, less fundamental and more controlling. Ownership rather than family. "Does that mean they're tracking you?" Of course it did. I explored his edges past the walls I'd built, finding other, subtler shielding in place. How had I missed it? Too pissed off to pay attention. But no, not shielding, not exactly. A façade, like a fake front, built carefully to resemble the throne room of the mansion on the island where we'd discovered Femke. I glanced at Charlotte who nodded once.

"I'm taking care of it," she said. "Until Iosif can do it on his own. But he's learning quickly." At least he had some kind of training. That was a relief. She didn't ask me to remove my wards around him so I left them in place, but with a touch to her she could pull them down when she felt he was ready. So like me to fly off the handle and assume no one else could take care of things. I should have known Charlotte was already managing this new problem with her usual quiet awesomeness.

Still, I wasn't so sure Iosif eventually being in control of his own magic was a good thing or not, but let it go for now. We'd have a talk about responsibility and personal gain later, Iosif and me. A long and detailed discussion.

"How do you know they all survived?" This might not have to be a giant mess after all. They'd been around for a while and hadn't really caused any trouble outside the kidnapping of Femke. But the fact they were choosing to interfere now made me shake off my complacency about them. Clearly the Black Souls had an agenda and I couldn't have them crashing my party before I was able to finish what I'd started and...

And. Wreck what was left of the Universe. Maybe they thought acting against me was saving themselves? I could hardly blame them, I guess.

Iosif's hands danced like they had lives of his own, first tapping fingertips together, then wringing, then settling into a white knuckled ball on his jittery lap. I was almost mesmerized by their activity as he went on.

"When I was allowed into the inner circle," he said, awe and fear in his voice beyond what he'd shared so far, "there was a ceremony." He swallowed hard and I caught a glimpse of a massive, dark cavern, bodies in black robes.

The scent of smoke, flames climbing from a central brazier. Iosif himself standing, sweating, over a naked young man who wept and begged for his life in Russian. Any good feelings I had toward the small mafia man burned up in a wisp of fury as I glared at him and understood where his woken power came from. And how they'd accomplished it. Iosif must have seen the imminent death on my face because he squeaked faintly and his ever active hands raised once more, a wall between us, his weak sorcery writhing in an attempt to protect him. "They did the deed," he said, "before I could stop them." Tears rose in his eyes and he wiped at his mouth once more, chin dropping, doubling over the collar of his shirt. "It was horrible." Okay, fair enough. Stripping the power of another being and taking it for your own had a certain taint to it that you could never scrub away. I felt it then, but admitted to myself Iosif seemed genuinely disgusted by the source of his magic and let him live.

For now.

"Are these Black Souls a threat to the completion of Creator's statue?" I'd forgotten Oliver was with me, my blond shadow speaking up. His deep voice sounded almost impatient though when I met his eyes he seemed concerned. For me?

I shrugged, stood up, suddenly needing to pace, to let out the pent up energy that woke the moment he interrupted. "Maybe," I said. "If they are working with Belaisle." I spun back to Iosif. "Are they?"

He seemed confused, eager to help but unable to answer. "Who?"

"Liander Belaisle." I shot an image of my nemesis into the small man's head, not even trying to be kind or gentle about it. Iosif recoiled but didn't seem angry or hurt, even as a lightbulb of understanding illuminated his expression. He even managed a shaky smile, like he finally had something truly valuable to share.

"Yes! I've seen this man." He nodded with overeager enthusiasm, the thin strands of his comb over wavering in the air. "He was never named to me, but he has been in conversation with my bosses."

"There's your answer." I crossed my arms over my chest and started up into gray eyes that met mine as an equal. "We have to deal with this. I need to know if they are planning anything that could interfere. For all we know, they possess the last two pieces."

Iosif choked a laugh, though there was no humor in it. "I wish you the best of luck."

My returning glare could have cut steel. "We don't need luck," I said. "We have inside help, Iosif."

A soft wail escaped him and he half stood before my power slammed him back down into his seat.

"Information," he gasped. "I am happy to supply information. All that you require. But I beg you, please."

He choked on his words before speaking again. "They will kill me. Worse than kill me."

"So will I," Charlotte said, so casually it made her statement all the more horrible. The hairs on the backs of my arms stood at attention as the wolf in her let Iosif process his fate.

Yes, I felt sorry for him, briefly. Rocks and hard places and frying pans and fires… ah, the clichés could spin on for days. But he was in this with us, like it or not. And I had no doubt whatever horrors the Black Souls could lay on Iosif, he hadn't seen the final moments of the end of Andre Dumont. Just the briefest flash of memory made bile rise in the back of my throat, the scent of decay and the liquidation of flesh as vivid as if I was still there, watching Andre melt to death.

"I will uncover what you need to know." Danilo had remained silent the entire conversation, though the former wereking's twitching and faint grunts in response to our talks weren't lost on me. He surged to his feet, tall, wide shouldered body filling out again from the lean, failed werewolf I'd freed from the WCP prison. While a far cry from the robust ruler I used to know and admire, he seemed even more dangerous now. "Iosif will be immensely helpful. Or he won't."

The mafia man squeaked.

"I'll leave you to handle it then." Oliver was right. Sure, the Black Souls might be an issue, but I had no proof they were. And all Iosif had been able to do was confirm what I already knew about Femke. I was the first to admit I had a habit of going looking for trouble. Mind you, it was one of their number who'd done this thing to Femke in the first place. Around and around my head spun. Until I finally did my best to just shrug it off and let others handle it. Aside from layering on more bad news, this trip had been a giant waste of time.

"I beg you," Iosif said as I turned away, ready to go. "Just kill me now." I glanced back over my shoulder at him as the werewolves surrounded him. He ignored them, staring at me with utter terror on his face. "I would rather die than go against the Black Souls."

There is an option, Oliver sent. *You could give him white sorcery. That would at least grant him an edge and perhaps a backbone.* He sounded faintly disgusted and amused at the same time under his concern.

I thought about it for a heartbeat before rejecting the idea. *He's a survivor,* I sent back as I shrugged to the little man. *And he has Charlotte and Danilo to look after him.* I just hoped I wasn't sending them all to more danger than I understood. Still, I had to trust they could handle it for me, for Femke. Charlotte knew better than to hold back if she needed me.

"Don't take any stupid risks," I said to the werequeen who grinned like that was funny.

"We'll be in touch," she said, waving me off. She'd

really taken this whole monarch role seriously. I tried not to be offended by being dismissed and stepped through the veil to the sound of Iosif babbling desperately in Russian.

There is one issue, Charlotte sent as I departed, a faint hint of her own worry in her wolf. *Oleksander has sensed the mafia sniffing around the palace.*

Her grandfather, former wereking himself, wasn't one to panic or even voice concern without good reason. *Contact Piers*, I sent, the veil closing behind me. *He and the sorcerers will help you.*

Already done. She paused. *Thank you for trusting we can handle this on our own.*

If only she knew I just didn't have the energy to deal with it. *Just be careful and keep in touch.*

Her wolf's snort of derision cut off as she let me go.

EIGHT

I was all for heading right to Hong Kong, but to my surprise Oliver's power butted up against mine and paused us in the veil, holding me there with gentle insistence.

He didn't apologize, and I had a feeling asking was new to him. How odd to deal with someone who didn't fear me or act uncomfortable in my presence because of who I was. Sure, my family loved me, my friends, too. But no one ever really treated me like they were my equal. Even Max acted more like a caring father than a partner and Quaid had proven to me our relationship had never been one of equals despite what I might have told myself to the contrary.

And my beloved Liam… I wouldn't go there. Not right now. Not with the handsome soldier in my presence, making me think of my heart when I really didn't have time for such nonsense.

Says you, my demon grumbled.

Since when is love nonsense? My vampire sounded sad.

So jaded these days. Shaylee turned her back on me. *I'm disappointed.*

Sigh.

Rather than try to placate the girls or find an excuse to leave and end this conversation before it began, I allowed myself to hover there in the thinning membrane between the planes of the Universe still left to us and waited for Oliver to speak.

You seem to spread yourself thin, he sent at last. Not a judgment, more a curiosity. *I find that fascinating and wonder where your motivations lie.*

He'd never questioned me before, not really. Aside from gentle teasing and occasionally poking his nose in to ask for clarity, he usually just watched and kept his mouth shut. Maybe he'd simply been trying to figure me out.

Fair enough, though I fought the urge to know more about him in return. Blamed my demon for the zing of interest and didn't listen when she chuckled evilly in the back of my mind.

You sound like Max did once upon a time. I did my best not to sigh over that. Small things, right? *Why do my motivations matter, anyway? I get the job done. That's the ultimate truth of things.*

Oliver waited, head tilted to one side, gray eyes calm

and quiet.

Fine.

The thing about small stuff, I sent, *is that the tiniest of situations tend, in my experience, to blow up into gigantic monstrosities of disastrous mayhem when I'm not looking.*

He laughed, the sound ringing in my head, white teeth flashing against his tanned skin as he nodded, blond hair bobbing in the silent space of the veil.

I get it, he sent. *But why do you feel so compelled to deal with things yourself when you have so many competent and passionate people who want to help?*

What do you think I just did? Irritation woke, prickled me with the first hints of anger. Didn't help the veil cried out to me in its unique voice, its pain reaching me, guilt worse than any hurt. But it wasn't just me in here, reacting to being questioned for my actions. I snarled at my demon when she made herself known through the burning of my emotion and felt her retreat in sullen silence.

Ultimately, Oliver sent, tone light as if he didn't care if I was pissed at him or not. Genuinely didn't give a crap. How refreshing. *But you were ready to run off and solve everyone's problems yet again. You seem to have a hero complex, Sydlynn Hayle.*

Snarl. Okay, my demon could come out now. Except she sniffed at me and, like Shaylee, turned her back in vexed silence. Fine. I could handle this alone. *And you don't?* I tossed my head, jabbing Oliver in the chest with one index finger, feeling the tightness of his skin, the hard plate of muscle beneath. My demon whispered something suggestive and highly inappropriate over her shoulder that would have made me blush if I'd let it. The traitor. *I seem to recall someone throwing himself heroically into his own death to save a damsel in distress. And her dragon.*

Oliver laughed again, a deep, resonating chuckle this time, filling my mind with the deliciousness of it. Faint light twinkled in his gray eyes, lit with sparks of green. Damn him, why did he have to be so yumtastic? It was a distraction, pure and simple. *Some dragons are worth dying for.* He winked. And *their damsels.*

Oh, no he did *not* just flirt with me. Not here and now on the edge of the end of everything with the dying Universe aching around me through the touch of the unhappy veil. He did not get to stir those kinds of feelings when I really, really needed to put Creator and Her fate first. Nor did he get to distract me and get the girls wound up in the possibility this might turn into something. Did *not. You do realize what I do is none of your damned business?* Okay, so I hoped he'd get mad, snap back. And admitted when I reached for a fight it was my go to. That I just used Quaid tactics against him without even thinking about it. The sudden need to have a rip roar bit at my heels like an angry dog.

But Oliver just shrugged, carefree and full of that

loose joy that seemed to follow him around everywhere. *Like it or not, what you do is everyone's business. Doombringer.* His hand rose, finger extended. And, eyes tight with laugher, he booped me on the nose.

Booped me. On the *nose*.

Before I could show him the error of his ways with the amount of force I deemed necessary to drive him back to his own Universe, Oliver looked away, absent expression endearing enough it saved his sorry ass from destruction. For now. I was angry at myself for letting him get to me, for choosing old habits instead of applying fresh eyes and feelings to this man who was nothing like anyone I'd ever known. Instead, I did my best not to admire his strong profile. Or the way his body filled out his plaid button up loose over a white t-shirt, the snug fit of his jeans, the casual way he ran his big hand over the side of his jaw.

Just one bite, my demon whispered as Shaylee sighed. *He'll forgive us.*

Grumble, mumble.

I admire you, really I do. Oliver looked back, a grim smile in place of the open good humor he'd shown. *I'm not questioning your heroism, Syd. Quite the contrary, in fact.* It was clear he had no desire to stroke my ego, and yet I felt my anger ebb at his words. Then surge back in response to my response. If twisting me into knots without trying was going to be the norm in our relationship, I'd be walking.

Relationship, hmmm? My demon's snarky prod just made things worse.

I think she likes him, Shaylee giggled.

My vampire's sigh made me want to hug her.

Oliver went on, oblivious—at least I hoped so—to the running commentary in my head. *I'm wondering how I can be more like you.* Not a trace of embarrassment came with that pronouncement, no ego of his own or manly bluster. Like he had no idea what that was. Just simple admiration that had the exact effect on me I expected from him. Stupid pale skin. Showed my blushing. But Oliver went on as if he never noticed. *I've often felt there was a massive flaw in my people*, he said, mental voice soft, almost embracing me but with hesitation he might be rejected. Such an odd mix, this man. Equal measure of confidence and caring, pride and casual acceptance of his own imperfection. Could I ever find such balance?

Dreaming again, I see, my demon snorted.

She had to say it.

We are trained from birth to build our power, Oliver sent. *To use those around us to gain more. I was taught from birth to treat my fellow Order soldiers like stepping stones. Even my mother, my siblings.* He shook his head again, sighed. *I always thought going against such thinking meant there was something wrong with me. It's been enlightening to see such a different way of being. And gives me hope for the future of my own race.* He paused, pursed his lips. *If any of us have a future, that is.*

I reached out on impulse and took his hand, the warmth of it, the faint roughness of his palm, the way his big fingers curled around mine in a gentle but accepting grip. There was no sadness in him, not really. More an opening, an understanding, which reached me like no other attempt could have. I forgot the teasing, the girl's taunts and jokes. The very fact he wasn't trying was the winning factor. And softened me to him against my better judgment.

Finally, my demon sent.

Just kiss him already, Shaylee giggled.

Girls, my vampire sent. *Patience.*

I exhaled into the soft agony of the veil, felt it hiccup softly in sorrowful response. This was the first time I'd spent any time here since its pain became a burden, since it started calling to me to save it. I'd done my best to block it out, knowing there was nothing I could do. But hovering here, with Oliver's hand in mine, my own heart open, I reached for the veil and felt it hug me back.

There, you see? Oliver laughed again. *Everyone loves you.*

Why that word? It was just a word, though, right? Didn't mean anything. Four letters strung together. Might as well be a nothing word. Uh-huh. I shrugged and pretended it didn't affect me, grinned like love was no big deal even as I quivered inside like a giddy teenager who thought the popular boy liked me. Seriously. *Not everyone.*

He winked, tugged on my hand, his own power linking to the veil. *I know it's hard to trust me*, he sent. Actually, the opposite. I had to fight not to trust him. But held my peace as he went on. *I want to be one of those people you rely on. Who can do for you what you don't have time to do. Who you can count on when you are called on to be Doombringer.* So much intensity suddenly, more than I'd ever seen in him, sensed in him. I shivered from the touch of his magic, not out of fear or worry or stress but sheer attraction.

Delicious. His magic, his body, his heart. Everything. Yumtasticly nomazing. And absolutely out of the question.

Instead of answering I opened the veil, the familiar feel of Hong Kong on the other side. Oliver didn't comment, didn't seem unhappy or frustrated either. Instead, he left his offer open, hanging between us, as I carefully concealed our presence and pulled him behind me out of the place between planes and into the living room of the head of the WPC Enforcers.

NINE

And realized, the blush still on my face as we stepped out into a familiar living room, this was the worst possible place to bring Oliver after the conversation we'd just had. Especially considering the girls continued to remind me with their own desires how deeply affected I was by his presence.

Dear elements, I just had to bring him to see my ex in that state of mind, didn't I? And while no one else may have felt the awkwardness, I was acutely aware of the dull heat inside me at the brief touch of Oliver's hand on my shoulder even as the man who'd once shared my bed and my life observed the intimate exchange.

Intimate to me, anyway. Surely the brush of the soldier's fingers on my t-shirt appeared like a casual accident to someone outside our previous conversation? From the tightness around Quaid's eyes, that was far from the case. Which stirred my irritation and cleared my head. Bless him for being a jealous jerk when he didn't have the right.

Speaking of which, Payten was home, her giant boobs and bulging belly an affront to my own bruised heart.

Classy all the way, right?

Okay, deep breath. Yes, I was a grown up. Yes, there would be a time I had to get over the whole Payten/Quaid situation and stop letting it bother me. And I would, I promised myself that. But in times of frustration or high alert the old, cranky me liked to latch onto hurts as reminders I was still at least that human. Pathetic, sure thing. But oddly, such prods to my ego kept me grounded.

Ethie's reaction at our appearance only increased my detachment from my feelings for Oliver as my daughter, fury written in her blue eyes, stood from where she ate her breakfast and, jaw jutting forward in aggressive dislike, tossed her dark curls.

"I'm not hungry anymore," she said, stomping off to slam her bedroom door behind her.

"Remind you of anyone?" Quaid's smirk cut deep. He might have thought he was being funny, but my daughter's rejection hurt me more than I could say. He must have known he'd stepped over the line the moment he spoke because his smile dropped and he looked away, clearing his throat.

"Coffee?" Payten's voice held that chipper, bright tone people used when they were fighting desperately to keep a situation from turning into a crapshow. Instead of pounding my ex into the ground and leaving behind a bloody pulp for being his normal, everyday jerkasaurus self, I decided on caffeine. And peace.

For now. There'd be time later to contemplate if it was worth continuing to make this a thing or just let it the hell go already.

Quaid was careful not to stare at Oliver as we sat down at his kitchen table overlooking Hong Kong harbor with three cups of coffee and my heart in my throat.

"I'm sorry about Ethie." Payten's hands slid over her gravid belly beneath her flowing, blue dress as she leaned with a weary expression against the counter, her face pale and drawn. I chalked it up to late stage pregnancy, the twins likely giving her some grief at this point. Hard enough carrying one baby with magic at a time. Two? I think I would have chosen to sleep out the final month if my daughter had been doubled up inside me. Gabriel had been a dream, but Ethie... well, she was as much trouble on the outside as she'd been on the inside. Typical Hayle, actually.

I waved off Payten's excuse, feeling weird still about the whole situation. The fact it had been about eight months since I divorced Quaid, that the pregnancy coincided with my departure to live with the drach, still rankled. My fault. I'd made that choice. Opened my ex up to falling face first into his present situation. Still. Way to wait a day or so before banging his old flame and knocking her up. Said a lot for our relationship in the first place.

Sigh. I really had to get over this already.

Oliver's quiet half smile for the tired witch was kinder than I could have managed. He quickly rose and offered her the empty chair, pulling it out for her while her husband grimaced. Likely because he should have done it first. The way he looked at Oliver and then at me made me realize I wasn't the only one feeling awkward.

Well, we were all adults and had crap to handle. So we'd just have to suck this up, wouldn't we?

"This isn't a social call." Quaid's normally deep voice emerged gruff and edged in annoyance. He looked tired, too, though I knew his weariness came from his own caregiving, that of controlling and keeping Femke from melting down before we could save her from the soul inside her. I filled him in on what Iosif told me while my ex-husband's face paled in horror and his new wife covered her mouth with one hand, eyes wide. Her chest heaved, her already sizeable breasts now swollen as she neared her due date, still a way out but close enough she looked like she carried two melons over a basketball everywhere she went. Yes, uncharitable of me, I know. Still.

Humanity called and I allowed it an ego stroke.

"We have to deal with the Black Souls." Quaid half stood before falling back into his seat with a groan. "But we need Femke to act officially."

"Maybe not." Oliver spoke up before I could, his mind going down the same path mine seemed to be travelling. "The Sorcerers League would be far more appropriate an organization to investigate, would they not?" Of course. Piers. We could bypass Femke for now, at least. Though there would come a time when we'd have to do something about the WPC leader. Something either permanent helping or permanent removing. I didn't like to think the latter might be necessary.

Quaid grunted, shook his head. Chose not to confirm Oliver was right. Instead, he took a stab at me. "So kidnapping her had nothing to do with you after all."

Wow, thanks for that. Considering I'd been blaming myself, too, I took his words as a personal insult. "Probably both," I admitted grudgingly. "Though now it seems they were more interested in finding a way to shut down the ability of the WPC to act against them." I hadn't seen it and that bothered me. A lot. Enough to make me want to break someone.

"Can't you just remove Femke from power?" Oliver's reasonable question made things worse, if only because it came from him. After all, we were all thinking it, weren't we? All of us at that table, including the pale and shaking

Payten. But Quaid snapped anyway, likely out of his own guilt. I knew how he felt.

"If they are controlling her," he growled, "they've been careful enough to paint inside the lines. She's done nothing to warrant calling for her removal. In fact, everything she's ordered has fallen within the parameters of the WPC's mandate." He was right about that. Even interfering as she did with Mom and the North American Council had been instigated by the other territorial leaders who demanded the new council system Mom put into place be reversed. Imagine their dismay when my mother had given every coven in her territory equal say and rights. No wonder they freaked out.

"But we know better." Oliver nodded, shrugged, clearly unaffected by Quaid's irritation. "So we have two options then." From my ex's scowl the "we" Oliver was throwing around made him furious. "Find a way to remove the tainted soul from Femke or displace her one way or another."

I didn't like the sound of that. Neither did Quaid, and the gasp from Payten told me she assumed the same meaning the three of us shared. I stared in shock at Oliver who seemed surprised by our attention—my horror, Quaid's fury and Payten's hurt—and then raised both hands as Iosif had so recently to ward off our reaction.

"I'm sorry," he said, gentle, kind. "While you may think little of my people and our ways, I didn't mean kill her."

Okay then. Quaid didn't settle down, still bristling. Before he could freak out on the Order soldier, I leaned in and took my ex's hand. The moment I did, the fraction of white sorcery I offered up slid inside him and bonded to his darker power. Quaid's anger drained out of him, some of the deep weariness leaving his face, his eyes as his newfound strength buoyed him and gave him respite.

"I should have done that ages ago," I said. "Just never seemed like the right time."

Quaid nodded grimly, though it took a long moment before he removed his hand from mine. What was he thinking just then? Did it matter? From the pain in Payten's eyes, it did. But we were over, long done and gone, Quaid and me. I'd seen to that. And, in choosing her he'd made his bed, literally, and babies were soon to be the result.

His gaze settled on Oliver again. The big blond seemed amused suddenly. Not the best facial expression when my ex was still pissed. "You find this funny, do you?"

Oliver shrugged, one big hand around his coffee mug, the picture of calm and repose. "I find relationships funny," he said. "Our partners are chosen for us, combinations of power and lineage carefully tracked and charted." I didn't know that. Found it immensely sad as much as it rang familiar and oh-so-coven practical.

Considering I'd been forced into marriage myself when I probably wasn't ready for it, empathy for the souls caught in such a system wasn't a big stretch. "My own mother killed my father after I was born to ensure his power didn't go to another family line." She *what?* I'd met Shonya Opal. Formidable was one word I'd use for the massive redhead. Though a husband killer? I'd underestimated her drive for success.

Quaid swallowed and looked ill. "I pity your people, then."

Oliver looked back and forth between Quaid and me before sipping his coffee. "At least we are honest about how we feel," he said. Quietly enough it was hard to take offense but loud enough we were all meant to hear it.

Youch. And fair enough.

Tell me about it, my demon sent.

TEN

Payten turned her face away, cheeks bright red, silence falling over all of us. I knew his temper wouldn't hold quiet for long, but before Quaid could open his mouth, Oliver leaned forward and patted the pregnant witch's hand. She met his eyes with her wide gaze, eyes rimmed with moisture and he smiled. I knew that smile, dazzling and sweet, had been under its influence a time or two and knew the devastating effect it could have on a female heart.

"How are you feeling, Payten? The babies must be soon to come."

So much caring in his tone, genuine and focused. Like she was the only person in the room, all that mattered to him in that instant.

Jealous? I really was going to smack my demon if she didn't shut up already.

Payten smiled faintly back, as though forgetting the hurt of a moment ago. She rubbed at her belly again and only then did I realize her tiredness had an edge of constant pain to it. I'd misread her slowness for simple pregnancy issues. But was she having trouble? Quaid was too wrapped up in Femke and his irritation at Oliver to notice, I guess.

"I'm fine," Payten said. "Looking forward to holding them."

She's not well. Oliver sat back, still smiling. Such deep seated empathy—where did it come from in a man who just admitted to a cold hearted way of life?

I'll have the Kennecotts look into it. I'd have to remember. Would remember. Because despite what I might have thought of the two of them shacking up within minutes of me divorcing Quaid, in spite of our past and all the hurts and betrayals, she was the only steady Mom presence my daughter had in her life, something I couldn't give Ethie right now.

Quaid stood up, Payten trying to heave herself upright at his side but he waved her down, kissed her forehead as she sank back with a grateful sigh. "Let's go to Harvard," he said, turning to me at last, refusing to look at Oliver who had come to stand behind me in response to the Enforcer leader's move. "I need to see Miriam anyway. Maybe she can suggest something that makes more sense than removing Femke from power."

The dig did nothing to rile Oliver who laughed in my head.

He's a lot of fun, the Order soldier said as I opened a portal to the office in Massachusetts Hall where my mother kept court. *I can see what you loved about him.*

Don't push him so hard, I sent back as I waved at Mom across the veil, crossing at the same moment. She looked up from her desk, pinched expression unhappy. *He's under a lot of stress.*

All the more reason, Oliver sent, casual and airy. *To see how much he can handle.*

I smacked him with power, making him start. *I mean it*, I shot back. *This isn't a game, Oliver. Not some Order power play.* I glared up at him and he nodded as I finished. How odd his previous compassion for Payten in dichotomy to his torment of Quaid. *I care about these people. And I'll do anything to protect them.*

Sorry, he sent without a trace of embarrassment. *You're right. Old habits, Syd.*

Whatever. I left him standing at the doorway next to Quaid, the veil sliding shut behind them, and went to Mom to hug her. She'd risen from her chair, circled her desk and embraced me briefly, distracted and a little distant.

Let me help, I sent.

I wish you could, sweetheart. She sighed in my head but her attitude shifted and she managed a smile, a hug for

Quaid, too, and a nod of kindness for Oliver. "I take it this isn't a family reunion?"

"When have I ever bored you with the trivial?" I smiled wryly and sat down, diving into the pertinent details. Mom absorbed the story without flinching, though I saw her shoulders round forward slightly as she took on the weight of what I told her. Like mother, like daughter. One of these days I'd have to talk to her about the way the Hayle family accepted everyone else's crap as if it were our fault.

"Thank you for keeping me posted," she said. "I wish I could help you, but I'm afraid I have my own struggles to handle." Mom sat back in her chair, fingers rubbing at her temples, the throb of a single vein in the middle of her forehead sure sign of a headache. I slipped her some magic and felt her power embrace me back with gratitude.

"Anything we can do, Mom?" I'd never thought of my mother as weak or in need of assistance and today wasn't any different. But compassion for the ones I loved was hard to shed even when I, like her, had my own weight to carry.

"Sometimes," she said, voice thick with frustration, "I wonder how we survived as a race." Her anger surfaced, bubbled a moment and then fell away when she smiled again, with more vigor at least. "I'd like to take them and collectively knock their heads together."

Knew the feeling, had considered it myself a time or

two. "The new council setup still giving you trouble?"

Mom stood, went to the window and stared out into the early fall evening. Darkness had already engulfed the campus, Harvard Yard lit with artificial light. We'd just come from breakfast in Hong Kong, bright sun washing through tall windows. The time zone shifts always messed with my head. It took a moment to adjust. But there was no missing her tone, no mistaking the touch of her power despite my disorientation. When Mom spoke again, she sounded the most tired I'd ever heard her. "They're willingness to work together lasted about ten minutes, as I suspected. But the dissolution of the Hensley coven has worsened the issue." My fault, and yet it had to be done. "They're breaking into camps, leaders taking sides. Old school against new school and those opposed to Tallah and those for. It's a free for all and they're cutting me out of it." She looked back to me. "I'm losing control of them, Syd. And I fear when the dust settles we may not like how this story ends."

"If the story gets to end." Oliver's compassion came through loud and clear. "If Syd's destiny unfolds quickly they may not have a chance to break apart."

Miriam laughed, brittle but with a hint of humor. "I'm not sure if you understand empathy yet, my dear. You're supposed to try to make me feel better, Oliver. Not worse."

He laughed in return, kind, genuine, free of

awkwardness or self-conscious judgment at his error. "Sorry. I'll do better next time."

But it seemed his offering had done the job. Mom was smiling again, and this time with sparkle in her eyes, her old good nature returned.

"I'll deal with it," she said. "And if they implode, so be it. It will be on their heads." She nodded once, sharp and decisive and I sent a quick, hard hug of magic to Oliver.

Thank you.

You care, he sent. *So I care.*

Quaid looked annoyed and I grinned at him in spite of myself. He could be as irritated as he wanted. Now he had moved on to his new life I had to find backup I could count on. Okay, not entirely fair. He had his own messes to deal with, namely the giant one that was Femke. However, I wasn't about to cut him slack. Not when we were all having bad days lately. And when, ever, had he had my back without a fight first?

My attempt to hide my snark just made him angrier, yup yup.

Before Quaid could shoot off some comment that ruined the mood, someone knocked on the door to the office, a soft touch of magic interrupting. Mom's power opened the door and I stood to greet the one witch that right now wasn't on my crap list.

Karyn Barrett let out a low cry of happiness and

hugged me tight, her blonde bangs hanging over blue eyes bright with tears. When she pulled back she wiped at her cheeks, hands shaking where they gripped my upper arms.

"Syd," she said. "I'm so glad you're here." She glanced over my shoulder with a smile of apology for Mom. "Nice to see you, Miriam."

Mom waved off her sentiment. "What's wrong, Karyn?"

"It's Pender," she said, meeting my eyes again, lips trembling around a brave smile. "He's asking for you, Syd."

That couldn't have been the reason for her sadness. "What happened?"

She shook her head, gaze falling before she heaved a shaky sigh. "Sorry," she whispered. "We've grown so fond of him since he came to us. It's hard to say goodbye."

Where was he going? When she looked up and into my eyes again, I understood like a thunderclap hit me across the head.

"Be prepared," she said. "Pender is dying."

ELEVEN

"Since when?" I grasped at Karyn's hands and she squeezed back, the two of us locked in a moment only we could share. I'd left him in her care not so long ago. The old Enforcer leader had been discovered by some of her witches after suffering in the not-so-tender mercies of the Brotherhood. He'd been abandoned, broken, insane, dumped on the streets of her city. When her people found him they'd taken him home to her and she'd cared for him personally since then. I'd only seen him once, the day he called me Doombringer. Had won a moment of seeming lucidity from him. But, from what she'd told me along the way he'd never recovered. If anything, from the sounds of what she was telling me now, he was only getting worse.

"Syd," she said, soft and full of understanding, "I know about Tallah, why you did it." She might as well have punched me in the stomach. I wasn't expecting to talk about this with her, not right now. But she seemed insistent she be allowed to get out the words she had to say so I held still and listened. "Please know I'm not mad, that I would never judge. I understand, many of us do." She seemed to hesitate a moment before pushing on. "Tallah lost our trust a long time ago and you, you have always been there for us. So, if you say she betrayed us, we believe you."

We. The Shadow Council maybe? The ones who had come to me when Mom was reinstated as the leader of the NAWC and asked me to lead an alternate council, one that watchdogged my mother's efforts?

"She aligned herself with Jean Marc Dumont and the Brotherhood." It was so important suddenly Karyn hear the full story but she was nodding and squeezing my hands again.

"We know," she said. "I know. You did what we all would have done in your place." She glanced over my shoulder at Mom. "There are those of us who stand with you, Miriam. I want you to know if the time comes you're not alone."

The relief on my mother's face made me want to hug Karyn all over again. In her usual Hayle witch style, Mom inclined her head with queenly graciousness. "Thank you," she said as if Karyn's assistance and backing wasn't necessary but absolutely welcome.

Only my mother could pull that attitude off and get away with it. Well. And maybe the smiling young coven leader standing in front of me. Her eyes sparked with magic as she winked at Mom who winked back.

"Damn the Hensley sisters for putting us in this position." Karyn let my hands go, her own sliding into the pockets of her pale blue overcoat. Only then did I notice there were beads of moisture on her shoulders, in her hair. She'd come from the rain, it seemed. "I've done my best to be the voice of reason and, from the show of support I've received in your name, I have about two thirds of the covens ready to come to the table."

Mom's eyes widened. "I had no idea."

Karyn flushed, stammered, then straightened her shoulders as I smiled at her. "I'm sorry for speaking for you without your permission but it seemed the right thing to do."

"It was." Mom came around her desk and joined us, kissing Karyn gently on the cheek. "Well done."

This one will do, she sent to me.

Succession material. I'd thought so for ages.

We'll see. Mom's voice sounded more chipper than it had in a long time. "Tell us about dear Pender. What does he want from Syd?"

Karyn shrugged, sad all over again. "I don't know," she said, "but he insists. And he's fading so fast I hate to disappoint him."

"Let's go," I said, hugging Mom before waving off Quaid. "Go home to Hong Kong," I said, "and keep doing your best. I'll be in touch."

His scowl responded with its usual unhappiness. "We still haven't answered the question of Femke. Don't make me run around the plane following you only to brush me off, Syd. This is important." He flinched then, glanced at Mom, at Karyn, guilt on his face.

I didn't have to tell him Pender's life was equally so. Femke had waited this long. She could hang in a little while longer.

"Then stop following me," I said. And winced inwardly. Might as well have slapped him. *I can't solve all of your problems,* I sent. Yikes, I really was losing my tact and any sense of kindness with him. *You can do this, Quaid.*

His magic shrugged me off, turned its back on me. *I'd expect that from you,* he sent in return. *Go, do what you want. We'll cope without you.*

Maybe I deserved that burn. And maybe he was feeling far more pressured than he showed. Regardless, I let him have his angry jabs and cuts and simply shut him out.

I left him there with my mother, Oliver in my wake, Quaid forcibly removed from my thoughts. Instead, I focused on how glad I was to know Mom had more support than she thought but worried I was going to something that would break my heart.

His hand was limp in mine, pale skin thinned out to transparency, the bluish veins barely pumping blood through roping coils that pulsed visibly, slowly, in time with his laboring heart. I tried to push magic into Pender Tremere, to support his failing systems, his own power retreating softly in my wake, hiding like it knew what was coming.

It didn't help, not even when I tried to share white sorcery with him. The flame of pale power flickered and went out with a hiccup of apology. His breath caught and held a moment, thin chest not rising again for far longer than it should have taken for him to draw another lungful of air.

Karyn was right, hadn't pulled the punch to the gut that was the emaciated creature in the bed beside me. Pender wasn't a young man by any means, but nor was he ancient and withered. At least, he hadn't appeared so until now. Beneath the thin sheet he was a long, lean bundle of sticks inside a wrinkled sack of leather. He snorted softly as he finally breathed again, nose elongated in his thinness, dark circles burying his eyes deep in their sockets. His teeth stood out against his line drawn lips, Adam's apple bobbing in time with the stuttering last effort of the heart inside his sunken chest.

The air smelled old, despite the open window, the fresh sheets and comforter, the jar of wildflowers by the bed. Death clung to Pender with knowing hands, ready to take him from us when the time was right. But he wasn't ready to go yet, not when his fingers tightened on mine with purpose and his eyes finally opened.

Though we'd had our differences in the past—mostly thanks to rules he was forced to uphold—Pender had always, in the time I'd known him, striven to do the right thing. No matter his personal beliefs, justice and the law had been his two upholding principles and I could never fault him for those. But the man who looked at me through those dull, hazel eyes wasn't the powerful if occasionally ineffectual Enforcer leader I'd first met. Instead, a shattered and crazy man peered at me with as much joy as he could muster under the circumstances of his failing body.

"Syd," he whispered, lips cracking, tongue washed out to gray as it swept shakily over his mouth and caught at a droplet of blood forming in the separation of skin. I healed the damage with a touch of energy, eased his pain as best I could while tears filled the corners of his eyes and the holes there, the deep pockets making his gaze seem to float behind a pane of glass.

"Pender." I squeezed his hand gently, a lump in my throat. I hadn't expected to feel this much sympathy, this heavy loss for his passing. But he had been a part of my life for a long time for better or worse. And had suffered too much for me not to feel this way.

"It's almost done, isn't it?" That sounded lucid enough. He giggled faintly, the effort seeming to drain him and allowing finally the gathered moisture to run down the sides of his temples and onto the pillow. I stroked at the tears and nodded.

"Almost," I said. "You can't stay to see it through?"

He shook his head, the barest of motions. "The Universe calls me home," he said, the words without strength, more read from the movement of his lips than heard. "I can't wait. She promised I could go first."

She? "Who, Pender?" Why was I here? The last time he revealed my new identity to me, the one Belaisle reaffirmed. Doombringer. Did Pender have more information from Creator I needed to know? Or, was he simply calling out to me in his last moments because he wanted me with him? And, did it matter which?

She's here, Pender sent, his mental voice stronger than his physical one, though distant and full of holes. As though he were already almost gone. I held onto him. *She's always here.* He showed me an image of the veil and, at last, of the statue of Creator. *She promised, if I was strong enough. If I just held on while they hurt me. I did, Syd. I held on.* It seemed so important to him I know that. I nodded as he went on though I didn't understand, chalked it up to babbling and madness. *I did as She asked. And I'm ready.*

Interesting. Oliver's comment jarred me out of my sorrow and irritated me. He soothed my mind with a gentle touch before going on as if he hadn't just interrupted a private moment. *Does She speak to you?*

She does, Pender sent, mind smiling as I felt him reaching past me, outward into the darkness, entire being outstretched. *She has a message.*

This was the most together he'd been since his discovery as a homeless man by the Barrett coven. And had to be important after all. If Oliver hadn't prodded him, prodded me, would I have let this go? Maybe. *What did she tell you?* Oliver knew better than to ask that question, leaving it to me.

It's all up to you now, Syd. Pender's voice sounded like his old one, like the man I used to know. Even his eyes seemed to focus more sharply, his soul returning for a moment to face me as the Enforcer leader he once was. *When the time comes, you must let go and do what is necessary. The blood spilled is on your hands, but it is on all of ours. And that doorways are meant to be closed so new ones can be opened.*

I shook my head. *I don't understand.*

Pender's sigh caught me off guard. *Neither do I*, he sent. *But She wanted you to know.* And suddenly he was drifting, faster and faster and I couldn't hold onto him. *I've never seen so clearly*, he sent from a great distance, leaving me behind. I felt the pull of the void. His spirit, converting to that magic, was being drawn into the place where the Universe fell. *Belaisle's torture and Dark Brother's mind... they've freed me, Syd.* I remembered the touch of

Creator's sibling, His horrible deconstruction of my mind and soul and body and shuddered as Pender went on. *Please. Trust yourself. You're doing it right. He'll tell you when it's time. And he's the perfect one for the job.*

I didn't get to ask who he was talking about, could only assume it was Oliver, when Pender's spirit lifted from his body in a whisper of sound much like an exhalation of breath. I continued to hold his hand, tears trickling down my cheeks. He waved to me as the void, a dark blot in the air around us, opened up and swallowed his soul.

He was smiling when he vanished. I wished that brought me comfort. But as he died, the veil shrank further with him, weeping as it went, matching my own tears and I could only sit there and pat his cooling hand, the shell of who Pender had been all that remained, feeling the veil die with him.

Not completely. But enough it was hard to let him go, to look up and wipe away my tears even as I felt the air magic of this plane and the Universe go with Pender Tremere along with a giant chunk of the veil out there beyond my ability to save it.

It's almost done. Oliver's hands settled gently on my shoulders and drew me up, away from the still body. Karyn and her family took my place while my tall, blond friend—and he was my friend, I knew that to the bottom of my heart—pulled me kindly and firmly against him so

I could hug him tight and let someone else carry the weight for a minute.

But only a minute. I couldn't bear hearing them cry, seeing Karyn bend forward and kiss Pender's forehead. Too much loss for one lifetime. And I had so many more lifetimes to go. How depressing.

Saved by the boy child. Gabriel's mind reached mine as I finally pulled free of Oliver and wiped my nose with the back of my hand.

Mom. He sounded like he knew what happened.

Sweets. I hugged him with magic. *What's up?*

Good news and bad news. His grim tone told me more the latter than the former. *You'd better come.*

Happy to. Anything to escape the mourning family and their fallen adopted son I suddenly felt like I'd failed somewhere along the way.

TWELVE

Gabriel and Max waited for me in the underchamber of the Stronghold, Jiao and Sass with them. I avoided the drach leader's eyes, if only to evade for a moment the remaining sorrow there. His missing wings seemed even more obvious when I pretended they weren't gone. That he was whole again in body. Still, despite his lingering loss, he carried himself like the drach lord he was, so I refused to belittle his efforts to hold up a good front by feeling pity.

Sass embraced me, his power as familiar as ever if his shape as a human still took some getting used to.

I'm sorry about Pender, he whispered in my mind.

Me, too. I shook off my sadness. "Okay, sweets." I turned to Gabriel who watched me with sad eyes. "Spill the bad news."

He grinned past his worry about me, though there

wasn't much happiness in his expression. "That's what I love about you, Mom," he said. "No pulling punches." He glanced up at Max who nodded slowly before my son sighed and shrugged. It was nice to see Max up and around again, to observe the massive shape of his drach form around him despite everything. I could almost pretend he was whole again. Dark Brother's unforgivable command to have Max's wings removed still ached inside me like a hurt I'd never heal so I could only imagine how he felt. I tried to reach for his mind, unable to stop myself from wanting to comfort him despite knowing better. Pender's loss must have weakened my determination to treat Max like nothing changed when everything had. But he blocked me out, if kindly.

Another time, the lord of the drach sent, distant and quieter than usual. *I'm quite functional despite my disability.* It made things worse, somehow, him bringing it up with such calm and dignity. *When this is done and we can comfort each other.*

Fair enough, if troubling. I wanted to ask him if they knew yet why his wings refused to return. I'd broached the question to Oliver days ago when Mabel admitted despite Max's recovery and the efforts of the Stronghold to save him, his wings refused to sprout. The Order soldier had no answers, however, and unless we were willing to cross back to the Dark Universe—not me, not even for that—we'd just have to figure it out on our own.

I should have just done it, gone and kicked drachmor ass, found an answer. Told myself it was my dedication to the Universe and Creator that kept me here. I couldn't risk screwing up the plan. But knew better. Pure terror held me in my Universe. I just hoped Max could forgive me that.

Part of me noticed the subtle changes, the way he shied from me as never before, how he seemed to hide who he was from the world around him. Still, he had the right to his healing time and of all people I knew better than to push him.

He'll be fine, Jiao sent. *Wings or no wings*. Such fierce devotion. Yes, she was his apprentice, tied to him with magic. But she loved him in her own way, I had no doubt. And, if I knew her at all, was beating herself up over his loss as much as I was. *I'm watching him.*

Before I could respond, Max's mind bumped both of ours. *I'm not an invalid*, he sent. *And my hearing is in no way altered by my lack of flight capability.*

Good to know, she sent, crisp and sarcastic. *That your eavesdropping tendencies weren't damaged.*

I had a feeling this back and forth had been going on without me and decided Max's apprentice had things well in hand. Instead of putting myself in the middle of their little battle, I focused on my son and prayed my drach friend would find a way to come back to us fully. "Hit me."

Gabriel let me into his mind and, instantly, I realized he'd been in the veil again. Before I could freak out and give him a piece of my combined demon/witch/Sidhe/vampire/Mom anger to chew on, he shook his head at me, the starry distance of darkness showing in his gaze and stopping my tongue.

"It doesn't matter," he said, voice deepening, layered over with the hum of the veil and the Universe behind it. "Please listen. We're running out of time."

So he'd said before. Gritting my teeth against a response I just nodded, not trusting myself to say anything that didn't involve go to your room to one of the most powerful beings in the Universe.

Considering said Universe was rapidly disappearing, maybe I could have gotten away with it after all.

"I've searched the remainder of the veil and planes for the last pieces," he said. So distant, so cold as though the boy he was faded into the Universe itself.

"That's not what you told me earlier," I said. Snippy? Okay, so I wasn't great at keeping my mouth shut or my irritation to myself. "Young man," I added for emphasis. Gateway or not, he was my son.

"Doombringer." Oliver said the name with some humor and when I turned on him to snark his grin cut me short. "Let the Gateway speak. Before the two of you in your infinite massiveness and power decide a family fight is more important than saving the rest of us."

Smartass soldier.

Gabriel grinned back, some of my son returning. "Thanks," he said. "I needed that." He sighed and shook himself, almost like a dog shedding water, before blinking his hazel eyes back into clarity. Sparks of green danced in them, more like his father than ever. I caught my breath and held it, sadness of losing Pender so soon tied to the end of Liam I couldn't bring myself to fight again.

"Any time you need a little grounding," Oliver said like he wasn't addressing a child of the Universe, "I'm your man." *Hear him out*, he sent to me, tight and private. *You know how hard this is on him.* Again with the surprise shift toward compassion. Would I ever understand under what criteria he doled out his caring? And wait just a damned second. Why was Oliver suddenly defending my son against me? Did he see something of himself in Gabriel? I knew the two had a few conversations neither would share with me, talks that had left them both grinning and growing closer to each other, but Gabriel was my son and I'd mother him all I wanted, thank you very much. *Without Gabriel*, Oliver went on, shattering my defensiveness with his words, *we wouldn't know what to do next. Where to go. What to look for.*

Damn him for being right.

"Okay," I said at last, letting out the remains of my anger, nodding to my son. "This is your show, Gateway. Doombringer at your service. You said you looked everywhere and they're not here. But you also said you found them?"

He nodded, all the confidence seeming to run out of him as he sagged and stuffed his hands in his jean pockets. Gabriel looked so young and vulnerable then, like my little boy at last, the one I wanted to pick up and cuddle, kiss his soft cheeks and rest my skin against his curling, blond hair with its streaks of red. To rock him like I used to when he was a baby and tell him I loved him, to protect him and keep him safe from such things as the destruction of the Universe and Dark Brother and the pending end of everything.

My son. What was I doing? And yet, this was Creator's choice and I had no say in it.

"I did find them," he said. "Though it took some doing. Because they aren't here anymore."

"Not the other Universe?" No way was I going back there, putting myself into the reach of Dark Brother again. The very idea made me break out into a cold sweat, shaky on knees that begged to buckle. Okay, so maybe I hadn't recovered from my encounter either. Max wasn't alone in that fact.

But Gabriel was shaking his head, looking grimmer than ever. "No," he said. "Not the other Universe." He hesitated so long I wanted to scream until he finally shrugged his thin shoulders so high his hands lifted free, arms swinging loose at his sides when they fell again.

"The void," he said. "The pieces are in the void."

He did *not* just say what I heard him say. I felt my entire body clench against that truth and shuddered. How were we supposed to retrieve them from a place that was no place at all? The few times I'd fallen into the void I'd almost become trapped there, only escaping through heroic measures of those around me, including the black ribbon that flexed on my wrist in sympathy.

I opened my mouth to voice my protest when my son's determined gaze silenced me. And horror dawned as I understood I wouldn't have to worry about getting in and out.

"Mom, retrieving them isn't your job," he said. "It's mine."

Oh, *double* hell to the *no way absolutely not never no way*.

"It's the only choice," he said, all reasonable like that was supposed to make me feel better or change my mind or wipe the surge of panic and desperate need from my pounding heart. "You can't do it, Mom. You'll be trapped and you're needed here." He held out one hand to me but I ignored his offer, his gesture as he went on. "I'm the Gateway. I can open a way to them and retrieve them directly, returning the same way."

My lips parted, my chest tight, the words I wanted to say perched on the tip of my tongue.

"Don't say no," he said, the Universe back in his eyes, in his voice, echoing in the underchamber. "I'm going and that's final."

I think my head exploded. It felt like that, if I'm going to be clinical about it. Boom. Fire, smoke, that kind of stuff. Weird how detached I became when it happened, like I stepped outside the raging body of the woman going nuclear as I observed just how red my cheeks became when I was really mad. How my eyes bulged so very much, the way my whole body took on this odd shaking that made me look like I needed a straitjacket. Or was creating a new dance craze. A bad one that people would create video memes out of.

I snapped back into my own body an instant later, just as my vampire firmly slapped me. Or, maybe it was that slap that did the deed. Regardless, I found myself panting and shaking as I stared at my son's defiance, the stubborn denial of the veil and Universe in his face, and drew a sobbing breath.

"Over my dead body," I said.

Oh, Syd, my vampire whispered.

Gabriel's jaw tightened. He'd adopted that teeth grinding thing from me.

"Sydlynn," Max started. And stopped, because that's as far as he got before I snapped my finger up and warned him to shut the hell up with a glare. He did as he was told. Smart drach.

"I'm not asking," Gabriel said. "And I stayed to tell you out of courtesy. Not to wait for your permission." He was already creating a Gateway, the form of it looming into life behind him. Black existed on the other side, just darkness and an empty feeling that left me breathless. "I'll be back with the pieces, Mom. And this will all be over at last." He turned, stepped into the archway, fearless and confident. While my mind and body and soul all tripped over each other and tried to reach him.

I was stopped abruptly by the force of power of several minds and was, instead, relegated to gaping as my son disappeared and his Gateway with him.

The silence after his departure hung around us all, heavy, growing weightier by the moment until I hoped it would crush them where they stood. The traitors. Sass's lips parted but I snarled at him and he shut up. Yes, that was good, just shut up already and let me ponder the demise of the people I trusted, who had held me back while my son, my Gabriel, went into the void from which only Mabel had ever truly escaped. And that barely.

Syd. Karyn Barrett's voice reached me, enough of an outsider from my little core of family she shut down my need to hurt someone and made me focus.

Karyn. Civil. Good for me.

I'm sorry this is so soon, she sent, reminding me with her mental touch she was still mourning Pender herself. *But I need your help. It's Shenka and Tallah. They're in California, at the old coven house.*

They were *what?*

They're stirring trouble. She paused, sad. *I thought you'd want to know.*

Someone to focus my fury on? I'd kiss her later. *Thank you*, I sent. *I'm on my way.*

THIRTEEN

The beach at Hensley house had grown crowded with witches already when I arrived, Oliver behind me, Sass and Jiao forcibly left behind with Max. I just didn't want them around me right now. Too bad I couldn't talk the lurking Order solider into staying with them but whatever. He wanted to see me in action? I'd show him action the likes of which the two sisters in question would regret for the rest of their short, painful lives.

Sand squeaked under the rubber soles of my sneakers, evening shadows falling over the shoreline. The scent of summer remained here, tried to calm me with its promise of better days. But I was long past such allure, drawn deep into fear for my son, anger for my mother, rage at the witches who lined the beach, focus elsewhere.

The Shadow Council. I should have realized they'd show up here, now, while Tallah stood on a large rock at the edge of the ocean and spoke to them with magic augmenting her voice.

I didn't want to listen. Was all for just plowing ahead and doing my bull in a fragile section act. But my vampire's power brought me up short.

Observation and planning, she sent. *Not your forte, typically. But wise, perhaps, in this circumstance?*

Only if we get to kill them after, my demon sent.

Slow and agonizing, Shaylee sniffed.

My vampire's chuckle wasn't helping any. *Bloodthirsty, princess? You?*

She shrugged inside me, earth power rumbling. *Blame it on demon.*

I'll take it, my demon sent with a grin.

Though I was accustomed to their running commentary, often going on in my head without my input, it was distracting enough in this instance I pulled up short, one hand on Oliver's arm, and decided to squelch my temper long enough to take my vampire's advice.

Shocking, she sent with a hint of humor.

Smartass.

I was sure I wasn't going to like what I would hear. But I at least needed to know how far Tallah had managed to screw things up before I ended her. I tuned in mid-speech and did my best not to lose it within her first few words. "The oppression of the NAWC can no longer be accepted." She sounded whiny to me, like a petulant child and not a firm, commanding leader. Helped ease my temper from pending volcanic explosion to simmering caldera of destruction. "We've been lied to and controlled for far too long, told what we can and can't do, made to feel inferior to witches whose only claim to power is their bloodlines." A few mutters of agreement, despite the fact Tallah's family were one of those, weren't they? At least, they had been once. She'd been part of that original council through her coven's connections. The fact she was spouting such lies only reinforced my belief I'd done the right thing taking her down.

However, despite her attempt to sway them, most of the leaders looked and felt pissed, including Karyn Barrett who made her way to the edge of the crowd and my side. Just as Tallah noticed I was there. She pointed in my direction, imperious and pompous. "Look, you see? The watchdog of your council leader has come to strip all of you of your power and covens, just like she did to me." More mutters, heads turned in my direction, a few who looked angry. But at me? From the wash of dislike, that was a yes. But not the wave of approval or support Tallah had been looking form, clearly, because she went on, a hint of desperation in her voice. "Will you let her take your families from you?" Instead of growing louder, she sounded sharper, harsher, like she was losing control of her speech. Her magic was no match, no equal for who she had been, the power of the Hensley coven long gone, dispersed, thanks to her. Like it or not, Tallah Hensley stood there because she screwed up.

"How about you tell us about Jean Marc Dumont and the Brotherhood?" I hadn't meant to speak up. I was just going to let her do her talking and then maybe kick her ass a bit before Mom showed up. Because Mom was coming, I could feel her. And she wasn't happy, nope, sure wasn't.

Tallah spluttered while Karyn spoke up. "Yes, Tallah," she said while the group swayed in response to her words as they hadn't to mine. "Explain to us about this alliance of yours with the very sorcerers who almost destroyed us." Heads turned, speculative looks reacted. There it was again, that wash of control like I'd felt in Scotland. So, Dark Brother was poking his nose in here, too? Or was Belaisle close by, monitoring the situation? Or, more likely, I was imagining things. That the stubborn, private and proud hearts of the witches gathered had created their own circle of pressure. Had made this moment one even they couldn't escape without help thanks to years and generations of fear. Karyn's magic pushed against them. And, though weakened like the rest, diminished without all the elements to buoy her, she succeeded in pushing back the curtain of deception they'd layered over themselves, answering that question for me. And confirming this spell they were under was of their own making.

Well, they were listening now, weren't they?

"Where's your proof?" That was Sashenka. I should have known she'd speak up for her sister, despite the fact I knew she was privy to the truth. Had been there when I'd uncovered Tallah's deception, had been furious with her former leader's betrayal.

Karyn ignored Shenka and went on as if she hadn't spoken. "Tell us how you thought any kind of association with the Brotherhood was a good idea, Tallah." Karyn's tirade had started as a question and was now a booming reprimand, the tone and push of a true leader, exactly what Tallah had been aiming for and yet fell so far from the mark. Way for Karyn to show her and the rest of them where she'd come up short. Despite my continuing anger, I could have grinning in pride at my friend's chutzpah. "And, while you're at it, tell us please why you blame Syd for protecting the rest of us from your insane plans to repeat Erica Plower's mistakes."

Tallah's response was met with a roar of approval for Karyn, drowning out the former coven leader's words as the web of control they'd cast upon themselves shattered and flew wide. Silenced a moment later as a wall of magic hit all of us when Mom and her Enforcers, Varity Rhodes in the lead, crashed our party in a wash of blue fire.

"This assembly has been called illegally." Mom's voice boomed overhead like a thunderstorm had taken us over, the power of the council pressing down, blocking escape for those who tried to flee. While it was still young and weakened like everyone else's thanks to the disintegration of the Universe, it was still far stronger than anyone here. Except me. And maybe Oliver. Still, I was glad I was on her side. I was about to reach out to her, to tell her she could tone back just a bit thanks to Karyn, when Mom spoke again. "Tallah Hensely, you are under arrest for invading territory to which you have been banned for life."

The coven leaders swayed, nervous and angry again. "I am protected by the World Paranormal Council," Tallah said, arrogance making her ugly. Making all of them ugly as their combined magicks formed a wall of solidarity.

Seriously? They forgot so easily?

"Were you in Hong Kong," Mom said, "I would take that into consideration. But you're in California, in my territory. And I won't stand for it." She gestured at Varity who hovered lower, touching down with a grim grin on her face. The other leaders didn't exactly protect Tallah with power, but neither did they move out of the way just yet. "Arrest her," Mom said, "for the safety of all witches."

"Wait!" Paula Santos spoke up, pushing her way to the front of the crowd. Her olive skin seemed darker than normal, black eyes snapping anger. At me? She could just stuff it. I eased forward myself, the others melting away from me and allowing me through, Karyn at my side and Oliver at my back. "We want to hear her out."

"Do you." Mom's unhappiness rarely showed, she was so good at the diplomacy thing. Far better than I ever was. But, at the moment, she didn't seem to care who knew she was pissed and let it out all over the poor Santos leader. "Then you'd like to be arrested along with her, I take it?"

Paula backed off, scowling, dark hair shining as she shook her head. "You can't do that. You have no cause."

"Anyone who supports a proven terrorist and traitor," Mom snapped, power crackling overhead in a show of blue lightning that made the entire collective of witches cry out in fear, "is fair game." The magic of the NAWC snarled in answer, reaching all of them equally. It was their power too, wasn't it? And it was on Mom's side 100%. Still, she wasn't doing herself any favors. Mind you, I'd been in her shoes a time or two and it seemed like a show of power was the only way to go when push came to crash bang boom. "Now, who wants to stand up for this criminal?"

"I will." I hadn't even noticed they'd appeared on the other side of the crowd, their entrance fanfare lost in the surge of Mom's rage. Femke's smile made my stomach ache, the grim way Quaid's face crumpled as he fought to control her proof enough to me this wasn't going to end well.

I needed to step in, to get between them, to end this before war broke out. Because it was coming, I could feel it. Like the ever-pounding tide behind me, a battle brewed, long unwaged. And I was terrified to find out who would win.

But my mother wasn't about to let me fight for her. She pushed me back even before I had a chance to act, knowing, I suppose, exactly what I was thinking and putting herself in harm's way.

"Is that so?" Mom's former anger had vanished, replaced with the polished calm I was so used to. If I was Femke—and she was in her right mind—I'd be scared. Angry Mom was bad enough. But composed, collected and professional Mom? They'd better run. Fast. Far. And not show their faces ever again.

"Release Tallah Hensley," Femke said. "She's under my protection."

"She's in my territory," Mom said, all calm and reasonable. Like Witchageddon wasn't pending in 3, 2, 1. "Making her my prisoner."

Femke's magic sparked, sending a cascade down to the sand beneath her where she hovered, glaring now. "Don't fight me on this, Miriam."

"Then stop sending this child to fight your battles for you," Mom said. "You want to take me on, Femke?" Oh. My. Swearword. *Mom*, I hissed in her mind. She ignored me and went on. "Then hit me, but do it personally. Otherwise, stay the hell out of my part of the world unless I call you."

Oh, no she did *not* just insult the leader of the WPC like that. *Mom*, I snapped again. What the hell are you doing? I could stop them all if they decided to tackle each other, right?

Right?

This was going downhill so fast I could barely catch my breath, power building on both sides, the coven leaders a third angle of the triangle as Mom and Femke proposed all-out war over a witch who should be dead already.

Let this go, I sent, tight and afraid. *She's nuts. You know that.*

Let me handle this, Mom shot at me. *Just have my back.*

Sigh. What could I possibly say to that? *Always.* I drew on my power and inhaled, ready for anything.

"Tallah Hensley has stepped over the last line of my patience," Mom said to Femke, power to power, Enforcer to Enforcer as their collective troops massed behind them, more joining every moment. "If you choose to protect her, I will have no choice but to petition the WPC to have you removed as leader, in conflict with the laws of our people."

Even Femke in her cracked state gaped at Mom for that. "How dare you?"

"How dare I?" Mom's repeat of her question came out cold and sharp. "I'm done, Femke. Push me. Just try it."

I have no idea what Femke would have done if Mom had prodded her further. Would they have really fought out here, in the open? Started a war no one would win? I think so. I'm pretty sure, in fact, that would have been the end of a great many things and people who mattered to me.

Didn't get to find out, as much as I would have liked—and been terrified—to see the end result. Instead, it was Varity Rhodes who acted next, who dropped from her hover beside Mom and strode forward, grasping for Tallah with her power and her hand.

"You're under arrest," she growled in her voice like crushed gravel.

Quaid swooped down, landing hard next to his old mentor, his hand on Tallah's other arm.

"Release her," he said.

They stood toe to toe, facing off over the furious form of the ex-leader of the Hensley coven who, naturally, focused her fury on the one person in the crowd she aimed all her blame at.

You guessed it.

She didn't speak, didn't warn me, just struck. And maybe, if she'd timed it right, if I wasn't aware of her hate, of the way she felt about me in that moment of truth, she might have gotten through, managed to hit me with magic, to do some damage. But I was ready for her, saw the real Tallah behind her eyes, the way she'd harbored all that resentment since the day we met, shown to me in her utter contempt and fury.

Tallah threw her power at me, every ounce of it, and it would have struck. Bounced from my shields, repelled or absorbed and I would have strode forward, maybe slapped her, maybe laughed in her face. But that attack didn't make it to me. Barely managed to leave her, blocked by someone who threw themselves in its path in an effort to save me, not knowing, I can only guess in that instant, Tallah could do me no harm.

Was it instinct that drove Varity forward? Was it the need to protect me, to do her duty, long years as an Enforcer too ingrained to allow her to stand by and let me take the brunt of that strike? I will never know. Only that the magical fury of Tallah Hensley, backed with enough sorcery it had chops and an edge only desperate hate possessed, lashed out and hit, point blank, the chest of the NAWC Enforcer Leader.

And there was nothing I could do to stop it.

FOURTEEN

Someone was screaming, maybe it was me, it sounded like Varity's name but I wasn't sure in the sudden uproar of sound surrounding me, crushing me as though its volume had mass and weight. My body was moving, I was sure of it, but everything was so slow, like the world had become stuck in thick toffee, dragging my feet, pulling everything back to a snail's crawl while the power burst in Varity's face and she staggered away.

Mom's expression turned down in such slow motion it was almost comical, Varity half turning toward me, her eyes rolling up in her head, mouth slack as she crumpled sideways and collapsed to the ground. My hands were pushing people out of the way, the shrieks turned muffled under the thundering of my ears, the beating of my heart louder than any other sound.

It took forever, a lifetime, to reach her, to stumble to

my knees, to grasp the old Enforcer leader by the front of her smoking robe while the gathered coven leaders swarmed in around me. Their power pressed into me, joining mine as we poured everything we had, in concert, directly into the limp and unresponsive body before me, every single witch of the council in attendance—Mom included, Oliver, too—giving of themselves to save Varity's life.

I knew before we started it was already too late, her spirit gone, devoured by the void but I kept trying, didn't I? I refused to quit past the sobbing that choked me, through the endless run of tears blinding me and making her dear old face waver in my sight, wetting her cheeks and the still smoldering velvet of her robe with the grief that poured out of me in an unrelenting stream. I have no idea when traitorous time returned to normal speed, ensuring she would never, ever come back to us. No clue when the others stopped trying, only that finally, with a heaving gasp of air of her own, my mother grasped me firmly in her grip—physical and magical—and pulled me free of my effort.

Gram was there, when had she come? I hadn't seen her in the crowd, though it made sense she'd be present, didn't it? I shook, shock burning a hole in me while I watched my grandmother cradle her friend in her lap and weep over her empty body, rocking her gently and stroking the short, steel gray curls from Varity's forehead.

I looked up, realizing from the sudden silence only a few seconds had passed, to see the pale, shaking form of my ex-husband staring at the lifeless body of his mentor. And, for the second time that day, was far too late to act.

He spun on Tallah Hensley with one goal in mind. I could see it on his face, read it in his posture. Knew him well enough to identify the murderous intent in his entire body and in his bubbling magic. I should have stopped him, moved faster, done what I could to protect her from him. Long after the fact I would wonder if I really wanted to save her. Or if I moved too slow on purpose.

I'll never really know, not unless I admit to myself if he hadn't killed her I would have done the job instead. But Quaid was moving, his Enforcer power gathered and, even as my mother choked out a cry to stop him, one hand raised from where she crouched next to me holding me against her, he struck with all the force of his position and magic.

Tallah seemed stunned by what she'd done and I knew the instant Quaid's attack flew she wouldn't survive. Defenseless in her own shock, she stared in mute acknowledgment and took the full brunt of his blow, just as Varity had hers. Sashenka screamed her sister's name, held back by a pair of coven leaders, while her sister rocked from the strike and fell to her knees, a hole the size of a basketball appearing as the center of her torso disintegrated under the blast of blue fire. Flesh sizzled a moment, a sigh escaping her in time to the wash of waves on the uncaring shore and Tallah toppled, face now serene, to her side, her hand falling on the hem of Varity's robe.

Offensive, that touch. I wanted to strike at her already dead body, to cleanse her filth from the old leader's clothing. It was Karyn Barrett who kicked Tallah's limp and lifeless hand from the black velvet, a look of utter disgust and hurt on her face.

Quaid turned, met my eyes, his own full of guilt and understanding. He knew what he'd done, I knew it. We all did. Not self-defense, no way to argue it. Acting out of malice and pure rage he'd committed murder in front of all of us. And though I would have taken his place if I could, it was he who shed his black robe to the sand of the now quiet beach as all the coven leaders stared in mute horror and Shenka wept over her sister's body.

"Quaid Moromond." Femke's voice crackled with power. No longer did he guard her, control her. The soul of Konstantin the sorcerer surged in her eyes, took over where once Quaid had fought to save her. "You are under arrest for the murder of Tallah Hensley."

They took him away though Mom protested, or tried to. Gone in a blink of an eye, Femke abandoning Tallah's body, Shenka's sobbing form, sweeping off to Hong Kong with my ex-husband in tow. Leaving the rest of us to stare at each other and try to make sense of what just happened. Less than a minute. Everything changed in less than sixty seconds.

Rage filled me, my old friend, taking me over, driving me to my feet. I needed to blame someone and Tallah was dead. So instead I turned on the collective, the damned Shadow Council and their meddling, their refusal to back my mother when they should have, their stupid infighting and camps and denial of their own self-worth.

And I gave it to them with both barrels.

"This," I said, jabbing my finger at Varity's dead body, voice low but carrying to every single one of them thanks to the vibrating power I let out. "This is your fault." They shook, shivered, tried to deny it but I held them there, forced them to look, to see, to comprehend what their damned backstabbing had done. "All you had to do was stand for something that mattered." Okay, simplifying things, but still. "Just have each other's backs." The ground under my feet rumbled as Shaylee added her own grief and fury to the mix, my demon snarling and pacing inside me. Even my vampire was shaken, hurt, flexing her power while the black blossom of my sorcery wound around the cool control of its white counterpart. "And now we've lost two who we couldn't stand to lose. Least of all now. All because of you." I shook them with power because I could, because I had to do something that didn't require slamming them all physically into the ground. Doing to them what Quaid had done to Tallah, what that horrible witch had done to the most amazing Enforcer I'd ever met. "Do you see now? DO YOU FINALLY SEE?" I didn't mean to shout but it roared from me at last, the sky overhead crackling as a bolt of lightning hit from nowhere, the acrid tang of its death in the air, the rumble of answering thunder deafening me and going on and on for a long time before I let it fade away.

"Go the hell home." I sagged, releasing them to the sound of sobbing as they slunk free, in ones and twos and small groups, hugging each other, regret real at least. I watched as they stopped and bent their heads to Varity's fallen form, paying homage though they didn't deserve even an instant of forgiveness, a heartbeat of grief. It hurt and helped in equal measure to rage at them, to let the anger fill the hole that her loss left behind. "And stop being assholes to each other."

Oliver was there and I let him hold me up, one hand gentle on my elbow, just a simple connection, enough to give me the strength to stand there and stare at the ground where the lightning had hit, the shining edges of glass created in the sand. I'd take it with me, use it to mark the place where Varity's bones would rest. A tribute to an amazing woman I would miss for the rest of my life.

"Our fault!" Shenka was on her feet, staggering toward me, silken hair tangled around her. No one had even acknowledged her sister's crumpled form, or Shenka herself. Garbage, cast aside. I could bring myself to feel nothing but contempt. I felt my insides tighten into knots, Oliver's grip firming up, a warning? No, just more support. "This is *your* fault!"

"How dare you." Mom's voice shook, the power of the council flaring beneath her as she dragged herself upright. Gram's fury matched my mother's, though she simply continued to hold Varity as Mom spoke again. "You selfish, petty child. How dare you?" Not like Mom to repeat herself. She was as floored as I was, I could only guess, out of any kind of craps to give.

Shenka shook, hands clutching at her upper arms as shock washed over her. She'd been like a sister to me, once. Tied to me with magic and friendship and love. Where had it all gone badly, turned to ashes and hate? When she'd chosen her lying sister over me.

"Family," she whispered, as though knowing where my head was, where Mom's was, likely. "Did you teach me nothing? Family is everything, Miriam Hayle."

Oh, no she did *not* throw that in my mother's face. The roar that emerged from me echoed back from the ocean, terrified sea birds flapping their way as fast as they could from the sound of my drach voice. I'd found it again, thought it lost to me with my wakening. Was grimly delighted that part of me remained and answered when I needed it.

Shenka flinched but didn't flee, her dark gaze now on

me. I could almost feel my drach form around me, my wings unfurling in the warm California evening, diamonds surely reflecting in my eyes as the first race that I shared blood with roared forth.

"Family," I spoke that word, the song of the drach in my tone, though not the warm, sweet, kind song. The battle hymn, the thrum of death pending. I was actually surprised the sky overhead didn't fill with the bodies of the drach at my reawakening. Not that I needed them. Instead, I pointed at Varity, focused on her fallen body, her empty shell. "Family comes in all shapes and sizes. And can revoke their privileges." This time I jabbed a finger at her sister's dead body, feeling fire stir in my belly, the need to shift and soar so powerful I knew scales likely showed on my skin.

Shenka didn't look at her sister. But she didn't relent, either. I'd had enough, more than enough, a million lifetimes of her. With my power tightly gathered out of fear of what I'd do to her, I turned my back on her and released the drach inside me, feeling her retreat with love and a murmur of regret.

"Sashenka Hensley," I said in as cold a tone as I could muster, "if I ever see you again, I'll finish what Quaid started and ensure the last of your bloodline doesn't see another day."

I felt her leave after a long moment of utter silence in which even nature seemed to hold her breath.

FIFTEEN

The family gathered, the small remains of the Rhodes coven receiving the body of their fallen sister with much weeping and embracing. Dagney Rhodes huddled next to Gram, the two with their arms around each other and I stayed out of it. My grandmother needed her witch sisters right now, needed to grieve while I felt the powerful urge to destroy something.

Karyn, a constant comfort, took possession of the angular chunk of shining glass as I laid it at her feet. Embedded within were the rippling colors of the magicks of our Universe in a glittering wash of shining splendor. The powers themselves might have been gone to the void, but even that couldn't stop the Universe from showing its grief for the loss of one so beloved.

I was tired of crying already and the grieving had only just begun. Karyn stood beside me, her hand somehow creeping into mine and staying there though I only noticed after the fact. My skin felt cold, bereft of life, much as the limp form of the fallen Varity. They'd covered the charred gap in her chest, though I'd seen it, would continue to remember it all the days of my life, as much as the gap in Tallah Quaid's fury left behind.

So much death. And it was only beginning for me, wasn't it? The renewal of my drach all the evidence I needed, though I knew ultimately this was my fate. Immortal, doomed to live a thousand lifetimes while those I loved and made a part of my existence left me, one at a time, from terrible circumstances or mundane. It was hard not to think of Pender as they carried Varity away, his loss tied to hers within me.

Mom went with her, Gram and Dagney, until it was just Karyn and me, Oliver at my back, standing outside on the front step of the Rhodes mansion in the crisp evening air so far from the warmth of California. I'd long given up on searching for meaning in the deaths of those I lost, instead doing my best to simply absorb the grief and move on.

Nothing I could do. No one I could call on and no hope of salvation for the dead. It was either push past it or curl up in a ball and never stop crying. And I had a job to do.

Karyn's lips pressed briefly to my cheek, almost hot compared to my own chill. I let her go, the lump in my throat a constant thing I'd have to deal with eventually. When I was sure I had myself under control, I turned and met his eyes by chance.

And fell into his waiting arms, Oliver's magic slipping around me, comforting me, pulling us into the veil so I could sob on his chest in peace.

Such comfort hovering there in the space between planes despite the thinness of its remaining touch, its own pain. It seemed to sense my grief and stilled, embracing me as much as the soldier who held me so gently, allowing me to pour out my loss completely without having to hold back.

When I finally released my death grip on Oliver's chest and eased away, snuffling into the dim quiet of the veil, I felt better than I had in a while. Not that I'd forgotten the end of Varity Rhodes or Pender Tremere or the fear for my son now lost in the void. Or, even, the fate of the very Universe in which I hovered. It was just that the simple kindness of the man before me and the pulse of warmth at my wrist helped hold me together, to breathe and calm and find level. The black ribbon embraced me with the familiar power of my drach heritage, reawakening my need to fly. It tied itself gently to the sorrow of the veil that grieved with me, made everything seem so connected I had to let go of the pain. I wasn't alone, as the girls within me so often reminded me. But it wasn't just their presence that kept me grounded, here and now. It was the truth that everything in creation had a tie to every other thing. And that truth washed the pain clean.

I managed a smile at Oliver, wavering and weak, but felt a bit of a laugh bubble up and let it out. *Sorry*, I sent.

Don't ever, he sent, *apologize for caring, Syd. It's what I love about you most.* I choked. There was that word again and not so casually tossed out, mentioned in passing. Focused on me, aimed in my direction. On purpose, with purpose. And, at last, as if finally reaching his own place of realization at what he'd said, Oliver blushed. Looked away, grin twisting his lips. *Now what?*

I sighed a heavy breath, knowing despite everything I still had a long way to go. *Quaid*, I sent. *Femke will execute him unless we do something.*

Oliver didn't hesitate, to his credit. *After you.*

I'd been to the WPC secure prison before, buried in a cliff side somewhere in Northern Ireland. In fact, I'd just been there, broken out one of their most notorious prisoners and sent him off with his sister in search of the Black Souls. I'm sure Femke was aware it was me who interfered with Danilo, though I had as yet to hear a word from her about it. Likely the Black Souls themselves were still trying to figure out what the former wereking's freedom meant to them. If they were controlling her, as I assumed they were, I had to worry about their motives more than hers at this point.

Sneaking in would be simplicity itself. But was I prepared to remove Quaid with force and hide him? It was a big decision. And not one I could make alone, I was willing to admit.

Mom. I hovered in the veil with Oliver tied in and reached for the only ally I could think of. She answered immediately, mind tired.

I know what you're thinking, she sent, her sorrow tied into the deep weariness in her voice. *I'm thinking the same thing. But Syd. We can't.*

Mom, she'll kill him. I had zero doubt. In fact, as I hung there, considering, my brain fired off a rocket of sudden fear and anxiety that grew by the moment into a ball of bubbling tension. *If she hasn't already.* I might not have been married to him anymore, but I couldn't bear another death. Not his. Not like this.

He's alive, she sent with so much assurance I unclenched and started breathing again. *And I'll see to it he remains so as long as I possibly can. But now it's up to you, Syd.* She sounded like she hated to deliver the ultimatum. *You have to find a way to help Femke. In her right mind she'll commute his sentence, I'm positive of it. As she is…* Mom didn't have to finish. *I have access to enough legal mumbo jumbo I can delay her for at least a few weeks. The old laws offer a sufficiently contradictory mess on the subject of witch murder I should be able to keep him alive for now.*

Good to know. Okay then. The Black Souls it was.

Except, my son. The end of the Universe. The pieces of Creator. If I had to think about it, my brain would explode.

One suggestion, Mom sent. *Payten and Ethie*. Now she sounded tense and I could feel her moving. She wasn't at Rhodes house anymore, but at Harvard again.

My heart stopped. Dear elements, his wife and babies. My daughter. Femke...

I'm on my way.

The veil tore willingly, practically hurtling me out of its rubbery membrane and into the quarters assigned to Quaid and his—and my—family. Just in time to see Payten, cornered with her hands clutching her belly, my daughter pressed to her legs, pinned down by a handful of Enforcers.

I know you know I'm known for my temper. It's never been something I've been able to control very well, no matter how hard I try. And considering the previous hour or so, it was a wonder I didn't just lose my crap and blow a giant hole in the side of the building.

Turned out, I wasn't the only one with a bit of an anger issue. Even as my demon spit out a swearword I won't ever repeat out loud and Shaylee grasped the base of the tower and shook it in rage, my vampire threw herself in a whip crack of spirit magic and lashed across the barrier of power the Enforcers raised to trap Payten and my daughter. Ethie's blue eyes widened, her tears stopping instantly as she took hold of the blade of white light with her own magic and jerked it sideways, cutting a neat line through the lineup of Enforcers. They fell as one, not dead—I'd had enough death—but unconscious, thudding to the floor while my daughter glared down at them, dashing her tears from her cheeks.

"Told you you'd regret it," she snarled before running to me and hugging me tight. I swept her into my arms, swinging her around, heart aching as she squeezed me back. "My mom kicked your ass."

I kissed her and laughed with bubbling nervousness. We'd been on the outs for so long I was shocked by her surging pride and love pouring over me. "The Hayle girls for the win."

Ethie laughed and nodded.

Payten staggered, drawing my attention as Oliver left me to support her. Face pale, she managed a little smile for him as he gently lifted her into his arms. "Quaid," she whispered.

"I'll tell you everything when you're safe." I gestured to Oliver who nodded, even as Payten cried out, a wet gush escaping between her legs, the hem of her dress suddenly soaked.

I froze at the sight, as her face washed out instantly to white, eyes rolling into the back of her head. She collapsed with a whimper into unconsciousness.

Not fluid, not her water breaking. But blood.

SIXTEEN

There was a time when I hated Payten, when I blamed her for coming between me and Quaid, a very long time ago. Okay, so not so long, maybe. But the instant I saw the blood I knew what it meant and realized her tiredness from earlier had nothing to do with stress and everything to do with the now struggling babies I felt crying out inside her.

My mom instincts drove me toward her, Ethie slipping from my arms as I blasted open the veil to the thundering sound of Enforcers breaking into the apartment. Femke's strident voice roared as I pushed Oliver, the gushing blood from Payten's womb slippery underfoot, through the gap in the veil.

"STOP!" She was too late, for once, and I was the one in action, sealing the way behind us while the membrane caught and rippled with the blast the WPC leader shot at our fleeing forms. The fact she'd tried to shoot me in the back wasn't lost on me but I had more important things to worry about. Three more important things.

We crashed into the kitchen in Wilding Springs, my daughter weeping openly, face crumpled in a red ball of terror. Tippy shrieking in her own fright at our appearance just as Donalda lurched forward, arms open, to take the now unconscious Payten from Oliver. He looked pale and shaken, though without a trace of embarrassment, and I felt his power detach from the pregnant witch when he let her go.

She's not going to make it. He looked ashamed then, his mind shoring up against me and the terrible thought.

Let me repeat a familiar sentiment I'd only recently shot at my son: over my dead body. No way was I letting Quaid's wife and babies die, not when I had the best healers in the Universe at my disposal. They were already on the way, I could feel them hurrying toward the house, and realized then Tippy, now under control and all business as she helped Donalda carry Payten at a half run from the kitchen, must have called them.

Lola and Thon Kennecott burst through the door, panic on their faces, freckles standing out on pale skin. I just pointed to the blood trail, followed behind them to the room that had been Gram's in my youth, the room where I thought she'd spend the rest of her life as a crazy lady, where she'd almost died and become a sorcerer instead. My daughter clung to my legs, still crying but silently, staring into the room rippling with magic and fear. Now Payten lay, gray and barely breathing, on the comforter, her dark blood soaking the coverlet while Tippy and Donalda backed off and let the twins in.

Help her. I didn't have to send that to them. Like their surging magic and expert ministrations already tackling Payten wasn't enough proof of their commitment. But Lola must have understood my panic and took an instant to reassure me, bless her.

We'll do everything we can. Why was there hesitation in her where once only powerful assurance came in the face of hurt and illness? I didn't have time to ponder it, not when Payten's life and those of her babies were slipping from us.

I needed to help them, to pour magic into the young woman's hemorrhaging body, but the moment I took a step forward I felt the blast against the edges of the Hayle territory and knew I had other issues to handle.

"Go," Lula snapped through clenched teeth, her hands glowing with blue fire. "There's no use saving her and the children if our territory falls."

True enough. Gram burst through the door in that moment, the Hayle coven power embracing me, her recent grief still etched on her face. But she took in Payten's presence, the blood and the pounding attack on the wards around the coven's territory in about a half a heartbeat.

"Let's show Femke Svennson she's not welcome here." Gram's grim tone and flashing eyes scared me more than she'd ever frightened me before. I raced after her as she stomped her way to the kitchen door. Paused with Ethie still holding onto me, staring up at me with hurt, loss, fear. I crouched, gripped her little arms in my hands.

"Baby," I said. "I'll be right back."

Fury lashed over her expression, tears drying in the face of my newest abandonment. She was right, maybe, to be so furious. I should have taken her with me. Her brother, after all, was out there, alone in the void, the Gateway. And she was the heir to the Hayle coven.

But she was my little girl, had seen so much already. I could keep one of them innocent a while longer, couldn't I? Knew it was the wrong decision the instant she jerked free of me and backed up a step, glaring. Hating me.

"I'll be with my mother," she said, before turning her back and running from the kitchen. Toward the room where Payten lay.

Syd. Gram's mental voice hit me, but not as hard as my daughter's ultimate rejection. I looked up, saw the regret in Oliver's face. But he knew better than to comment, to try to make me feel better. Nothing would help, not now. And I had a coven to save.

I ran outside, heart sobbing for my damaged daughter but power leaping forward to protect our family. Oliver joined me, following the blue fire arrow shot Gram's magic left behind, heading for the edge of her territory.

Syd. Mom's mind hit mine like a blow. *What's going on?*

Payten. I sent her a flash of what happened while Mom gasped. *Femke's here.*

Oh, no she is not. Mom cut me off, rage flaring. And I realized, as we touched down, Gram with a burst of flame so violent it singed her own wards from the inside, Femke and her collection of Enforcers were in for a very bad time of it. After all, they weren't just up against me this round. Nope. As I settled next to Gram, my power reinforcing hers while Femke battered the shielding from the other side, Mom appeared in a pop of power that made my ears ache.

This could end badly. Or, could just end. I held the two raging women at my side back with a whisper and spoke up, sarcastic amusement in my voice.

"Well, Femke?" I crossed my arms over my chest, the WPC Leader pausing, snarling as her power did nothing to break through. "Are you sure you want to do this?"

"Hand over the co-conspirator," she said, drawing herself up to her not inconsiderable height. She was thin, achingly so, and her normally blue gaze seemed tainted with darkness. But the Enforcers around her still obeyed her, not knowing she wasn't herself, that the sorcerer

Konstantin was running the show. When Femke shivered, I understood. She was still in there, wasn't she? Fighting with every single ounce of strength she had. The fight went out of me in that moment, the need to destroy. My friend deserved my help, not my hate.

"Come and get her." Gram's growl sounded more like Charlotte in mid-shift.

"You can try," I said, shrugging, all casual. "But, I ask you again. Are you sure? Because, you might think you know what you're up against. You may even think you can best one of us. But you've never had to face the full might of the Hayle family." Pride burst in my chest, my mother on one side, my grandmother on the other, the force of our combined wills pushing against Femke on the other side of the territory wards. Never mind the towering power of the Order soldier who simply stood back and observed for now. I had no doubt Oliver would step in if we needed him. We wouldn't. Still nice to have him there. "Trust me. You don't want to see what we're capable of."

Now, I sent. And shoved. Not alone. With the Hayle family power and the NAWC magic joining in, we took on the weight of the magic of the world.

And, to Femke's fury, we won. Eyes huge, face coated in a sheen of sweat from the strain, her Enforcers dropping like flies, Femke backed up a pace. Two. Until she and her people were left, panting and drained, twenty feet from where they started. I grinned at the deep grooves in the earth, the piled up masses of dirt behind them from the force of our repulsion. And shrugged.

"There's more where that came from." Mom tossed her head, flicking her fingers at Femke.

"Time for the WPC to mind their own damned business." Gram wasn't so gracious, slamming Femke full in the chest with power, so reminiscent of the deaths of Varity and Tallah I lost any trace of pride in what we'd accomplished. It didn't kill her, of course not. Gram wasn't a murderer. But it hurt Femke and the sorcerer soul inside her from the way her face twisted in pain at the blow.

"Go back to Hong Kong," I said. "The Hayle coven territory is off limits to all comers."

Femke hummed and Femke hawed and Femke stomped her feet. I cut her off audibly, pouring power into the shielding until she was simply a shaking, furious figure on the other side of the wall of magic. She said something I missed, pointed at me then herself before flaring into blue fire and vanishing, taking her Enforcers with her.

We didn't get to celebrate our victory, if that's what you'd call cutting off the territory from the rest of the plane. Not when Lula's mind grasped mine in desperation.

It's not working, she sent, her fear driving me back

toward the house with Mom and Gram on my heels, Oliver close behind. *Syd, she's dying!*

Payten's pulse had slowed so much I wasn't even sure she was alive by the time we returned to the room. Mom gently moved Lula aside, my daughter who clung with desperate need to the pregnant witch's limp hand. Lula wept while her brother, shoulders slumped, hugged her and rocked her.

Their power is diminished, Mom sent. *Without access to all of their magic they can't do their job.*

None of us can. Gram's grim expression hadn't changed.

That was what I felt in Lula. Sorrow, frustration, crushing defeat tried to distract me. But I was done losing. Our recent victory—short lived or not—against Femke gave me the kick in the pants I needed to shake off doubt.

Show me what to do. I reached for Lula's hand, sinking to the edge of the bed, feeling Payten's soul rising, knowing what was coming. And refused to allow it. Not on my watch. Her eyes flickered open, her mind reaching for me one last time.

Let me go, she sent. *And save the babies.*

I'd had another mother make that request of me, a brave and amazing werequeen I'd been unable to save. But I'd had enough loss for this time around, thank you. Was so over it. I grasped her hand and stuffed her soul back into her body, my vampire clinging to her to keep her inside while I jerked on the memories in Lula and Phon and channeled my power to let them use it.

Felt my daughter throw her power at me and took it, let her help me. The shining tears in her eyes told me I'd made the right choice at last, though I doubted such an act would heal the rift between us. Not by the power of her feeling for Payten.

Didn't matter. Not now, not yet, if ever. Lula was the first of the twins to grasp onto my magic, taking full advantage of all the tools I had to offer. To my surprise, even my demon didn't fight, resistance completely gone as the siblings took what they needed and gave it to Payten. And, in the process, I went one better and shared white sorcery with the dying woman and the two fading souls inside her belly.

With a cry of pain, Payten's body arched, the wet, tearing sound of her womb expelling her babies one of the best things I'd heard all day, followed by the plaintive and powerful cries of the newborn witches.

Stay, I whispered to her. *They need you.*

Stay, my vampire called.

Don't leave us, Shaylee sent.

You must remain. Even my demon. Even her.

And, though death called her, it wasn't answered, not that day, not that soul. Clinging to me, Payten chose life.

I wept over her while the babies cried.

SEVENTEEN

The armor is heavy on my shoulders but I barely feel it. I welcome it, in fact. It's kept me alive so far. The pressure of building power pushes against me, burning through the metal and scorching my skin, bruising my damaged body, crushing my chest so tight I have to fight for breath. I force my lungs to inflate out of sheer spite, scream in defiance, voice already parched and cracking.

My magic pulses, as weary as I am but refusing to quit as the massive wings of my friend beneath me sweep us forward, his power unrelenting.

We must reach them before it's too late.

The glowing, white sword of light hangs over my head, shining a beacon in our fore, casting shadows over the sharp, violent spikes adorning his once smooth, scaled shoulders. He is a weapon from the tip of his snout to the sharp edged blade of his tail, all of his creation now made for war. As mine is.

I clench tight the sword's hilt in my gauntlet as my mount's massive head arches backward, fire spouting in a cascade of heat and ash blowing past my cheek. My helmet is gone, I don't remember how, head ringing with the rush of impending death. It doesn't matter now. We're almost there, the building juggernaut of destructive force between the armies hurtling toward each other narrowing by the instant.

We soar into the barest crack that remains, the bellow of my companion the trigger for the power that bursts from us, the sword over my head erupting into a massive outward explosion of white sorcery devouring everything. I revel in it even as I embrace my true destiny. Doombringer. Light One. Wild Card of Creator.

Peace engulfs me while we die in the crushing press of the violent clash of their magic and ours.

I jerked awake, a soft snort of breath loud in the quiet air, my skin moist with sweat though I was just dreaming. I knew that dream, had lived it before, though this was only the second time it made its way into my rest.

It can't be a true foretelling. My demon's quiet statement shook me, if only because her usual bravado was nowhere to be felt. *Can it?*

It can, my vampire sent. *It is. The end of everything,*

A warning, perhaps, Shaylee sent, more poised than I expected. Deluded, but poised.

Or, my vampire sent, *I am correct and we are being permitted to see the final battle.*

I nodded, sinking further into the rocking chair at

Payten's bedside, a crick in my neck from the awkward position but unwilling to get up just yet. There was great comfort in the slow, steady back and forth of the old rocker, the swish of its rhythm, the creak of its hardwood bones. And I was still wrapped in the embrace of my death dream. There was peace in that ending. *That didn't feel like the Order attacking,* I sent. *I couldn't see them, could you?*

The armies? My vampire paused then mentally shrugged. *There were only the two powers coming together.*

Dark and Light, my demon sent, still subdued. *It has to be us and them, right?*

Don't jump to conclusions. How unlike Shaylee to sound so confident and to be the one to comfort us all. *From what we know we're just stress dreaming.* Like I said. Deluded.

But she faltered at that, relented even as I spoke. *It felt like a premonition,* I sent, hating to be the one to admit it.

Agreed, my vampire sent.

Fine, Shaylee sighed. *I give up, you're right.*

So, we're going to die when this is done. My demon actually perked, sounding more herself. *Well, at least we're taking the bastards with us.*

I could live with that.

No use in worrying about it right now. My vampire embraced us all as one of the two babies stirred in the bassinet at the side of the bed. I rose and went to her, touching her cheek with my fingertips, calming her tiny little soul with power. Her identical sister slept peacefully beside her. Twins were rare in witch families, often tied together in their power and none more so now than these two angels. I could feel the white sorcery filling them up, binding them together and wondered, in saving their lives, if I'd forever altered them.

For the better, my vampire sent, insistent.

That we can all agree to, my demon sent.

My, how adorable they are. Shaylee sighed over their crop of dark hair, their round faces and chubby hands. Premature by several weeks or not, they were both a fair size for their early arrival, and hearty.

You're welcome, little sweeties, my demon sent.

One of them hiccupped in answer.

The door eased open, a tall, familiar shadow falling over me. I sank back into the rocking chair as Oliver joined me, bending to take my place over the bassinet. His big hands reached inside, stroked at the soft hair on matching heads, their little cheeks, a tender smile on his face.

He looked up, caught me watching with, I have to admit, my own soft expression and blushed. Again. Becoming a habit for him lately.

You're wondering, he sent, sitting next to me on a wingback, arms crossing over his chest, one knee over the other, gray eyes full of laughter, *how someone like me can like kids?*

Crossed my mind, I sent. *Oh mighty Order soldier.*

He shrugged. *They're babies, Syd*, he said. *Who can resist babies?*

I grinned and sighed. *Thank you for all the help*, I sent. *Payten would be gone without you.*

I did my best. He frowned then, sank back, staring at her sleeping face a long moment. *But you were the one who saved her. I would have given up. And I'm ashamed to admit it.* He looked away again, meeting my eyes. *I've never been like the others, you know.*

Your people, you mean? He'd opened up once before, just a few hours ago, the first real insight I'd had into him. Had I won his trust, too? Enough he was finally willing to talk, I guess. And I was so tired from all the stress and loss and fighting, it was nice to sit there, rocking, listening to the clock in the hall chime midnight, and let him.

He nodded. *Do you have any idea how hard it is to pretend to be ruthless and careless, to find out at an early age you're not supposed to love your siblings but use them to get what you want?*

I can't imagine, I sent. I didn't mean to feel sorry for him and that wasn't what he was looking for, not by the way he waved off my sympathy.

I blame my mother. He shifted positions, hands folded behind his head. *I get it from her.*

I thought she was as driven as the rest of them? The idea that Commander Opal was anything but a powerful and practical soldier of the Order was almost laughable. And yet, she'd betrayed her master, hadn't she? Willingly took the side of her own Fate, Mia Dumont, the drach reviled by Dark Brother. Interesting.

Driven, yes, he sent. *But not for personal gain. To protect the people she cares about.* He sounded like caring about people was a foreign concept to the Order.

I understood that motivation pretty well. *What's the difference, you think?*

I don't know, he sent. *I've always thought I was odd, that something was wrong with me. Mom talked to me about it when I was really young, to try to save me from myself. Said her father did the same for her and his mother before him.*

Empathy passed down from generation to generation? That sounded off and more than a little suspicious. *Care to guess now what the cause is?*

I wish I knew. Though, it's tied to that theory about white sorcery I was telling you about.

Right. He'd been working on an idea, why he thought Dark Brother struggled to accept the new magic in town. *Talk it out, then.*

I'm wondering if there's a bloodline thing that makes me different. One person in each of my family's generations. He shrugged. *It's farfetched, I know, but now I've met you, been here for a while, farfetched seems more common than not.*

He could say that again. *Bloodline, huh?* I glanced down as the ribbon around my wrist flexed and grunted. Not because it hurt, but because the soul that was Max on the other side slid free of me and floated briefly to Oliver. He unwound his hands, sitting forward with awe on his face while the drach soul landed in his lap, humming softly before returning to me and winding around my wrist again.

Max. I met Oliver's startled eyes. *Is he of your bloodline?* I spoke directly to the ribbon. It burbled, spinning slightly before settling again. And opened its power to me.

Images flashed, of Max from the other side, young and fresh, clearly not my Max but close enough, and a beautiful redhead, pregnant. The power carrying forward from one person to the next, carefully guarded and protected, guided and nurtured, watched over and kept safe from Dark Brother and the Order. Faces flashed through my mind, faster and faster, lifetime after lifetime until it slowed, hit Shonya and then stopped on Oliver.

Why him? I sent directly to the ribbon. *Why now?*

Conduit, it whispered. Max whispered. I shivered at the sound, distant and soft.

To what?

To the Order. Oliver finished it, looking concerned all over again.

Yes. The ribbon didn't seem upset, though, simply settling into place again and falling silent.

Something we obviously don't need to beat ourselves up over, I sent.

Oliver's gray eyes seemed troubled, his face tight with strain. *You really believe that?*

I laughed in his head, shaking mine, sitting back again and watching Payten sleep. *I might not like it*, I sent, *but if I've learned anything, it's any effort I make to go against what I'm supposed to do just leads me to the same road, only with more bruises than were necessary.*

I'll take your word for it. Oliver sighed.

The ribbon flexed and I rubbed at it, had missed its presence there even just for a few seconds. Needing to connect, I sent a secret whisper. *I was worried you were going to him for good just now.* Not selfish or anything, right?

Never, the soul that was Max—and wasn't—answered. *I'm where I belong.*

Feel like chatting about that? But he had already fallen silent—no more "it", not now or ever—and I figured he'd only answer from now on if he felt like it.

I knew someone just like him. Snort.

Payten chose that moment to stir, inhaling softly, her breath disturbing the quiet. Oliver rose quickly and silently, waving to me before vanishing out the door, closing it behind him. I let him go, leaning in as the witch's eyes opened and Payten smiled at me.

"Syd," she whispered. "Thank you." And wept softly while I held her hand and tried to figure out what to say.

EIGHTEEN

Payten finally stopped crying, sniffling and wiping at her face with a trembling hand. I let her go long enough to fetch some tissues, helping her to dab at the tears, to blow her nose. She cried out softly at the pressure, the pain it caused, but laughed weakly when I winced.

"You know how this feels," she said, cheeks a healthier pink, honey gold hair looking far better than it had a right to after what she'd been through. I know I never looked this good only a few hours after having my kids.

I nodded past the envy. "Been there twice, done that, have the stretchmarks to prove it."

Payten sighed and sank back, gaze traveling to the bassinet, longing on her face. "The babies?"

I went to the basket, retrieved her first daughter, laying her out on Payten's chest with the tenderness of a mother and hurriedly went for the second. It was hard not to smile, to feel satisfaction and compassion for the joy on her face, the way she stroked her daughters and their soft cheeks, how the new tears were happy ones when she met my eyes.

Felt good. And I was on short supply of such feelings.

"They're beautiful." Her whisper sounded awed, her eyes lifting to mine briefly, so briefly, before locking on her twins again.

She was right. And everything took a back seat to this kind of beauty.

We sat for a long time admiring what she'd made with Quaid, my chest tight from a mix of emotions I'd never fully unwind from each other because I didn't want to. Sure, there was some old jealousy there, some new hurt. But Oliver was right about one thing. Who didn't love fresh life so precious and adorable? Forgiveness was born in times like this.

"Syd, I'm so sorry." Payten's words stumbled over each other. I tried to stop her, inwardly shying from what she had to say, but fell silent when her gaze begged me. She needed to have her say and though a part of me wanted to cling to the last of the anger I had toward her, I nodded and let her speak. "All of this is my fault. From day one."

"I think Quaid might have had something to do with it." I gestured at the girls and Payten giggled then fell still.

"Well, a bit," she said. "But I never intended for this to happen. I swear. I betrayed you once before, thanks to Ameline Benoit. No." She shook her head, frowning at her daughters, deep in thought. "Thanks to my jealousy, for wanting what you had." I already knew this part. She'd admitted as much to me, lost her place as an Enforcer trainee when then Leader Pender Tremere found out she'd been manipulated by my old enemy.

Water long washed under a bridge I'd burned personally.

Payten wasn't done, though. "You could have demanded I be punished far worse than I was," she said. "But you didn't. You let me go. I'll always be grateful for that." Little did she know how much I wanted her to suffer. But I had Quaid, thought I did. So I'd let it drop, moved on with my life. Until. "And it was you who kept us going, kept our spirits alive when the Brotherhood attacked." She flushed crimson. "I carried with me so much animosity, a longing for Quaid that never left me. But when I saw you at the Dumont mansion, I realized how petty and small I was being, had been all along. That you'd saved all of us and I'd done nothing but wretched things with my life." She sniffed softly, eyes shining. "I swore to myself then and there I'd never, ever, do anything to come between you."

I cleared my throat but she rushed on before I could stop her.

"It took all the strength I had to ask for help to leave the Dumonts..." she swallowed hard, hands clasping her daughters a little tighter. "You'll never know what you saved me from," she said. And I knew better than to push her further. Considering what kind of treatment Charlotte had received at the hands of the Dumonts, I could guess being a subservient witch in that household had to have been a nightmare. "I owe you so much, your mother, too, for taking me in the way she did. Without judgment or question." A tear trickled into her hair but she ignored it, eyes bright with gratitude I worried I wasn't worthy of somehow. "You saved my life. Gave me hope again. I'll never be able to repay you."

"You don't owe us anything," I said.

"I'd be dead or alone or worse," she said, firm, determined. "Not a mom to two gorgeous girls." She paused, swallowed. "But I did it, didn't I? The very thing I said I wouldn't do. I came between you." Tears choked her, genuine, clean.

Aw, hell.

"No," I said, finally admitting what I didn't want to say, admit, give voice. "No, you didn't. I did. He did. We did it to ourselves. We were never meant to be together, Payten." She stared at me with those huge eyes, mouth gaping open as I sighed and sagged, the girls quiet inside me. "We were broken long before you came along and no matter whether you'd shown up again or not Quaid and I wouldn't be married anymore." I knew it in my soul, understood it at its most fundamental truth.

Well done, my vampire whispered.

Payten's lower lip trembled, her cheeks red with emotion. "I'm so sorry," she said.

I nodded, accepting her words, grateful for them. "You're safe here, I want you to know that." Had decided that from the moment she'd arrived, bleeding, dying. She might not have been my favorite person once upon a time, but these precious bundles in her arms made her family, damn it.

Payten's face reddened further, her throat working as she fought off more tears. My own body reacted in sympathy, waterworks at the ready. How remarkable to find myself here in this position, actually kind of liking the woman I swore I'd always hold in contempt. But we'd all been through a lot, hadn't we? Made choices we regretted, done things we wished we could take back and redo or never think of again. And, now I was being honest with myself, Quaid had never really been mine.

"What will happen to us now?" She sounded like she didn't want to ask. Firmed her expression as she waited for the rejection I could only imagine she expected. Her husband was to be executed, her coven was gone and she was on the run from the WPC. It had to be a huge weight to carry. And I was familiar enough with world burdens to know facing an uncertain future with two tiny lives depending on you had to be as much a crushing pressure as watching the Universe fall apart.

The instant she asked her question, I reached for Gram, kicking myself for not doing it sooner. Felt my grandmother's instant, instinctual resistance and then reluctant agreement as I made a suggestion.

You're sure, girl? Gram's gruffness did nothing to hide her hurt. Varity. So soon. And yet, I'd seen how even she looked down on the precious twins after their birth, felt her fierce protectiveness rise at their arrival.

I am, I sent. *I'm asking.*

Granted, Gram sent.

I sat back with a smile when she reached for Payten personally.

I want to offer you a place in the Hayle coven. My grandmother sounded gracious at least, hiding her discomfort with the whole mess. Surely she didn't blame Payten, but then again Ethpeal Hayle was as good at holding grudges as I was. Who do you think I got it from? *Quaid's daughters deserve to be raised in safety and in love.*

Payten started crying again. *Thank you*, she sent. *We're honored.*

It only took a moment, the Hayle family magic linking Payten and the babies to the coven, embracing her as it recognized her tie to Quaid. It felt sad to me, a longing left behind. Did it have memory, know the woman it claimed as its own wasn't quite what it had been expecting? Of course it did. Because it brushed past me as it eased away, as if testing to see if I was still here.

The Hayle coven pledges to watch over and protect you, Gram sent.

My pledge to the family is my life. Payten completed the ceremony and settled back, her daughters stirring at the change.

I let Gram go, wishing I had better news for Payten. "Quaid is in custody."

She nodded. "I know. They told me he killed Tallah Hensley." Practical, quiet. "Why?"

"She killed Varity Rhodes." Just as practical and quiet. But Payten gasped at my admission, shook her head in horror.

"Syd, he'll blame himself forever." She swallowed hard. "He's always felt guilty over leaving your mother in a lurch despite knowing taking the WPC job was the right thing to do."

I'd once questioned that decision, but there wasn't much I could do about it now. "He couldn't have saved Varity," I said. "None of us could."

Admitting that, too, are you? My vampire's magic kissed me gently. *This night is full of revelations, apparently.*

"I won't ask you to risk yourself for him," she said. "Because I don't have to." She hesitated, as if struggling with what to say.

"You can't say it wrong," I said, understanding her

trouble.

Payten choked a laugh. "This will take some getting used to."

She can say that again. My demon groused but fell silent when Shaylee shushed her.

"His stupid pride will keep him from asking for help," she said in a rush. "But you can't let him die because he's an idiot."

I laughed, I couldn't help myself. She'd just described my ex so well I knew he'd made the right choice with her after all. "We totally agree on that much." My good humor faded some but didn't leave entirely. "He'll never forgive me if I interfere, Payten. He'll fight me on this, tell me it's justice, the law." She nodded, silent. As I shrugged and grinned again. "But he doesn't have to. I'll just have to take his martyrdom from him and make him choke on it." I leaned over and patted her hand, went further and kissed one of the babies. "He'll get over it, be okay after a bit, once he can sit with it. He'll have you three to take care of him."

The door opened before Payten could respond, Lula and Phon bustling inside. From their steady but professional smiles, I was about to be expelled. Instead of arguing, ready to escape anyway, I stood without being asked.

"Get some rest," I said, wincing at the silly platitude even as she smiled up at me with the tenderness of new motherhood. "I'll see you in a bit?"

Payten nodded, eyes glowing with tears. "Thank you, Syd. For everything."

I turned to go, only to run headlong into my daughter. How had I forgotten her in the shuffle and the dread and the pressure to save her stepmother? Ethie's previous return to adoring me had clearly gone out the window because she glared up at me with fury on her face. I'd left her behind once too often.

"Where's my dad?" Anger and fear and distrust all in a small, powerful package.

It made me suddenly remember my son was out there, on his own, in the void. And that I hadn't heard a word from him since he left only a few hours ago, that I'd forgotten about him in the drama of the last little while. It hit me with so much agony I struggled to speak, wanted to hug her all over again. I opened my mouth to explain, or try to, when she hit me with magic. Not hard, but enough to silence me and stir my anger.

"Go get him," she snarled. "Or don't come back."

"Young lady." Payten's chastisement came out less aggressively than mine would have, but seemed to work better. Ethie's face fell, her demeanor changing to hurt and lonely. I did that to her, I had no doubt. Created this volatile, damaged girl with too much power and arrogance for her own good. "You will not speak to your mother that way. Ever. Apologize and thank her for taking care of us."

"But!" Ethie stomped one seven year old foot. Wow, was I like this when I was her age? My anger was as natural as hers. Yup, I guess I was.

Mom deserved a medal.

"*Now*, Ethpeal." Payten's voice cracked. "You know your mother has the weight of the Universe on her shoulders. That she's doing everything she's doing for you, for all of us. And that no matter what happens, she loves you."

Why did that choke me up? The fact my daughter's step-mother was the one to reach her didn't help, fired up some old animosity. It didn't survive, burning out on its own and I was glad. This wasn't Payten's fault. I had to take full responsibility. I'd left my daughter behind. I know how I'd feel if I was in her tiny shoes. Especially with her brother taking up so much of my attention.

Was it always this way? Did I put Gabriel first because his father meant so much to me? Did my daughter sense that he was my—gulp, shame on me— favorite? Only because Liam was gone, though.

Right?

Ethie pushed past me, ignoring me entirely, climbing onto the bed and cuddling as best she could with Payten and the babies while Lula and Phone tended the weakened witch.

Syd, I'm sorry again. Payten sounded truly distressed.

She's struggling with understanding how important you are.

Just take care of her. I didn't mean to snap and softened my mental voice as I went on. *Please, if you can do anything for me, if we can call the ledger even. Just make sure my daughter is okay.*

Always, Payten sent, sad and quiet. *As if she's my own. Until you can come back to her.*

I left them there, wondering if such a thing would ever be possible. And terrified, suddenly, it wasn't.

NINETEEN

The bench in the back yard offered some comfort as it always did. But it felt different back here without the Wild Hunt slumbering under the earth, missing Sassafras's demon power wandering through the house. Sure, both had been gone for a while, the Wild permanently, Sass's loss more inconsistent. Not to mention I'd changed, more than I'd ever been willing to admit.

Blaming outside influences for my own alterations. How typical.

Surprise woke curiosity as I felt a mind touch mine. Tentative, nervous. As he should be for having the nerve to reach out to me here, now. After all that had happened between his family and mine. But Kristophe Dumont seemed changed, too, as I let him in to find out what he might possibly think was worth risking my wrath for.

Syd, he sent. *I need to speak to you.* Even his mental voice had a faint French accent. Reminded me of old times. Bad memories. The evil of his family. But I welcomed the youngest Dumont brother to join me anyway, opening the way for him to step through the gap in the veil I made, watching him as he stumbled out into the dark of the back yard and swallowed hard.

"I didn't expect you to bring me here," he said, voice shaking. Time hadn't been kind to the former teen heartthrob. While his older sibling had aged about as expected, still tall and broad shouldered with thick, dark hair, Kristophe's European model good looks failed him as he grew up. A paunch, barely hidden behind the silk button up he wore, spoke of soft living, his scalp visible through his thinning widow's peak. Lines etched his tired, pinched face, his eyes more sunken now. There was a time I would have felt satisfaction at how far he'd fallen. Right at the moment? Just sympathy, it turned out. Like Mia Dumont, he hadn't stood a chance in that wretched family.

And after the conversation I'd just had with Payten, I was in a forgiving and forgetting state of mind. At least, as long as he gave me reason to follow through.

"You wanted to talk." I shrugged, fearless of him, of who he'd been once. There was nothing he could do to me and I felt no threat in him. Was this a need to show bravado on my part, to prove to myself just how far I'd come? No, I didn't believe that as the nasty thought crossed my mind. I'd had enough negativity in the last little bit. And being with the babies had softened my edges enough I felt genuine curiosity without bitterness anymore. Besides, any antagonism he might have harbored was long gone, too. All that was left was his fear. The fact he was brave enough to reach out despite that anxiety was enough. I'd give him some credit to spend. And time to screw it up. "Talk."

He cleared his throat, hands shaking as he shoved them into the pockets of his dress pants. "You lost Jean Marc."

"If you mean let him go," I said, "you're right." Okay, not entirely accurate. But no way was I giving his brother the satisfaction of knowing I'd been forced into it.

No, not satisfaction. More fear. And not for me.

His face fell and he crumpled a bit. "I see," he said. "Then the information I have is useless."

Hang on a second. "You're done talking already? Really?" That came out with a healthy dose of sarcasm.

Kristophe's face twitched. Was that a smile? Dear elements, it was. "Maybe if someone would give me a second to get out what I'm trying to say."

I didn't mean to grin, but couldn't help it. Waved at him to go on. Refused after all to like another person who I'd vowed never to forgive in such a short space of time as Kristophe went on. Found myself doing it anyway.

"I know where he is." That came out in a rush. "If you want, I can help you find him." He swallowed, fear returning. But of me or Jean Marc? "I know you probably don't need my help. Unless you do." Cleverness. I'd always thought him the brainless one, the weaker. What intelligence had he hidden to mask himself from his family?

Interesting offer. "You're betraying your own brother?"

Kristophe's entire body twitched and he grunted something in French. "Not my brother anymore," he said with so much bitterness I sat up at last and paid attention.

"I'm listening."

"I don't think you understand how much I hate him." Spittle flew from his lips as he vented venom toward me, the tiny droplets caught in the light over the back door. He shuddered again and settled. "It's his fault, the failure of our family. His ambition, his greed for power. When Father..." He gulped, shook his head. "It doesn't matter anymore. I owe no loyalty to the Dumont family. To my dead father who was the end of us. Or to Jean Marc."

Maybe I should have felt empathy for him but all I could raise was pity. Would have to do.

"I get it," I said. "So, where is he?"

"In Russia," Kristophe said without hesitation. "With sorcerers known as the Black Souls."

Well now. Wasn't that a nice little bundle of holy

crap? Though, not so shocking, now I thought about it. Belaisle was in cahoots, had stolen the older Dumont from me. Made logical sense he'd dump Jean Marc in their laps, maybe. But to what purpose? And why would the Black Souls want the former Brotherhood leader?

"You're sure?" I had to talk to Charlotte. She'd want to know. And, maybe this could help their hunt. She had intimate knowledge of the Dumonts. Having Jean Marc with the ones we sought could help her locate him and them.

Kristophe nodded, face twisting in anger, impotent as it was. How frustrating for him. Okay, empathy. Fine. "He showed up. At my house, my new coven." Such rage, such stress and frustration in those words. "Boasting, just like always. That he was the most beloved, the favorite. He had no idea Father hated him." Bitterness burned me even from the distance between us. "He tried to recruit me." Kristophe's laughter sparked with pent up power. "But I'm done. I'm finished being his punching bag, his *chien*." My French wasn't great, but I knew at least the word for dog when I heard it.

This could still be a trick, my demon sent. *He could be thralled by Jean Marc to tell us this story. To lure us to him.*

I don't think so, Shaylee sent. She at least was sad for the fallen Dumont. *It feels real.* She hesitated. *He feels real.*

Of course it does, my vampire sent. *Which is why demon might be right. Layering a trap on truth is a perfect disguise for it.*

Still. She paused as Shaylee had done. *I believe him, Syd.*

And even if it is a trap, Shaylee sent, *it's not like we can't handle Jean Marc Dumont.*

But Charlotte and Danilo might be in trouble if they stumble into the nest without warning. My vampire sighed. *Families against their own,* she sent. *How tragic.*

I couldn't agree more. "Why are you telling me this, Kristophe?" Why now?

He slumped, turned half away, shoulders rounding forward, looking less pathetic and a fragment of the young man I used to despise and more wounded, near defeat. But, as yet, unbroken. Good for him. I fought his rise in my estimation as he went on. "I've met someone." Was that a ray of hope in him? A flicker of humanity? Well now. "He's helped me feel like my own person. For the first time." I instantly wondered if Jean Marc knew his brother was gay. I could only imagine the fury in Andre if he'd uncovered the truth. And allowed myself to feel, at last, kindness toward Kristophe, understanding. To spend his whole life hiding who he was from a cruel and terrible family who would never allow him to find happiness. Freed from that tyranny at last, changed by it. Only to face the chance any amount of joy he'd won could be ripped away again. He'd been a thorn in my side, yes. But if I knew anything it was motivation. And that people could change.

Deserved a second chance.

"Everything I've built, he threatens it." Kristophe dropped his hands to his sides, a plea on his face. "You owe me nothing, Syd. If anything, you should just send me packing. But please believe me. I know you have your reasons for letting him go. And that you want him brought down as badly as I do." He shrugged his narrow shoulders. "Or not, if you let him go. Whatever your reasoning, I know it has bigger implications than what matters to me." He shuddered. "I'd kill him myself if I had the courage."

Truth. "Go home, Kristophe," I said, slicing open the veil and waiting for him to step through to the other side, to the small bedroom showing through, the anxious face of the man waiting there. Older, a little, than Kristophe, bald and bespectacled. Dressed in tweed, of all things. A professor type, but with a kind and caring face. Real concern from his lover, aimed at me from across the distance. He raised one hand and I waved back, surprised at my own willingness to do so. Look at me being all friendly and stuff. Reinforced my new-found compassion. And my willingness to deal with the mess I'd let walk out of the Scottish castle earlier today. "I'll take care of it."

"*Merci*," Kristophe said with real relief in his voice. He even smiled. Saluted. And left me there to think, the veil closing on the sight of him hugging his lover.

That kind of tenderness was rare enough in my own life I envied him for the briefest of moments before I shook off the visit and searched for a familiar mind.

Charlotte. Her magic touched mine the instant I reached for her.

Here. I caught sight of her and Danilo in the forest, in wolf shape, snow softly falling around them. The scene was so peaceful as they came to a halt, panting into the early winter morning, I wished I was with them. *What do you need?*

I told her about Kristophe's visit and she pondered a moment before speaking.

You're far more understanding than I am, she sent. *And yet, Kristophe never did anything to me. At least, not like his father and brother.*

Is that forgiveness I sense, Charlotte? I couldn't help but prod her even though I knew exactly what she'd endured. The moment seemed to call for some levity.

She snorted back at me, the image of her wolf form puffing frost into the air making me smile. *As if*, she sent. *But the information is welcome. I'll use it to our advantage. Anything else?*

Just be careful, I sent, knowing it was useless and unnecessary but saying it anyway.

She didn't bother replying. Because Charlotte.

Yeah.

TWENTY

It wasn't long before Oliver joined me in the early October morning, such a contrast from the icy calm of the Ukrainian forest I'd sensed from Charlotte. His long sleeved button up was barely enough to ward off the cold for a normal person. Made me wonder in absent curiosity if he was like me in that regard. Though I knew a chill was in the air, was conscious of it, it had been a long time since temperature affected me aside from vague awareness.

He didn't try to speak, just sat with his hands in his lap, one foot over his knee, blond hair stirring occasionally in the faint breeze. As with the first time we'd sat here, I caught the scent of fabric softener—the brand the family had used for what felt like forever—and nature. But there was a metallic feel to him, too, that resisted my need to think of Liam. Where my love had felt like an oak tree with roots as deep as the earth, Oliver loomed more like a metal tower, running just as far beneath us, but without the softness and sigh of sap and leaves and bark. Not that he was hard or unrelenting. Just that his core had been hammered into place by a lifetime of rules and those who would use him for their own ends.

Tears tried to fall but I resisted them. Funny how quiet moments when I was actually free to sit and think triggered a wash of emotion like this. Then again, not so strange, I suppose. I was so used to action that the moment life gave me an instant to consider what had come to pass my body tried to shed the stress through crying or laughing or screaming at someone. Fair enough. I understood the premise, but I really didn't feel like losing it right now.

Later. When the Universe ended and there was nothing left to try to save. I'd fall apart and just be.

Oliver cleared his throat, startling me, before speaking with faint wonder in his voice. "Family," he said, "is complicated in your Universe."

I laughed, couldn't help it. Patted his hand before sighing and nodding, still smiling. "You have no idea what you've gotten yourself into."

He grinned in return. "Though I prefer yours to mine, Syd."

"Some days," I said, "I'd trade you." That was a lie. I couldn't imagine not having those I cared about to bully and prod and torment me the way they did. Tried not to think of the one person I cared about the most right now and where he'd gone. Failed miserably. And, at last, the tears won.

Oliver must have known where my head was. "He'll return," he said, gentle, kind, "and with what we need to see this to the end."

I nodded, wiping at the silent flow of moisture down my cheeks, wondering where the tight throat and burning chest was, why it was only the tears themselves that escaped. Those I could handle, as irritating as the wavering vision was, the wet on the backs of my hands. Speaking wasn't possible, though, not right now. Just in case words triggered the flood of other things I really didn't want to face just yet.

"I wish there was something I could do." I turned to see him frowning at his hands, frustration clear on his face. "I seem to be useless to you despite my desires to the contrary." I loved the way he spoke—okay, a strong word to use, but he let it out first and, well, there you go—so formal and yet as casual as anyone I knew. "There has to be a reason I'm here aside from causing your Universe to be at risk of invasion."

"And if that's exactly why you're here?" The idea hadn't been lost on me all this time. In fact, the thought crossed my mind more than once and, from the flinch of guilt on his face, the hurt in his gray eyes with their flecks of light, he'd been going down that road on his own without any help from me.

Oliver's mouth tightened, his gaze dropping again. "I won't betray you." Not a promise. More a litany. As if he'd been repeating it in his head for days now.

I thought of the black ribbon on my wrist, its admission about Oliver's bloodline. That he was a conduit to the Order. For what?

I reached out and squeezed his hand, felt his fingers wind around mine in a comforting grip despite his own anxiety. "You're here for whatever reason you're here," I said, accepting in that moment it was true. "And no matter what happens in the end, that's the way things are."

Oliver's mouth softened, eyes crinkling at the corners as his faint smile returned. "How wise and cryptic of you, Doombringer."

I arched an eyebrow, willing to play to lighten the mood. "All the better to confound and confuse you, soldier."

He sighed, fingers relaxing around mine, now simply in contact and not holding on. "Where do we go from here?"

I shrugged, knowing my time on this bench was limited, that the moment of respite couldn't go on much longer. But talking out the next steps felt like the right thing to do.

"So many options," I said, the overwhelm knocking me briefly into the back of the seat, washing me with weariness. "Mom needs my help, though maybe the mess with Tallah finally drove some sense into the coven leader's heads." Possible. Unlikely. I could hope. "Femke." Dear elements, Femke. She was unprotected now without... "Quaid." I'd have to break him out of prison, and fast. Femke wouldn't waste any time putting him to death, despite Mom's reassurances she was on the case. But where to take him that wouldn't put others at risk? And, ultimately, with the Universe falling apart, did it matter?

And, finally, I spoke his name. "Gabriel." Choked on it. Ah, there was the burning sensation in the corners of my eyes, the strangle hold of grief around my neck, the empty, sucking pit of despair in my gut. All for the sweet faced boy I loved with all my heart.

Oliver's fingers tightened again, this time to support me.

"I could go after him." I could, too. Easy enough to surrender to the void and fall within, to go searching for him. It had been such a long time—and really not all that long, honestly, less than twelve hours—since he left me, departing through the Gateway of his making, into the dark and the nothing.

"And do what?" Oliver wasn't arguing with me. He sounded genuinely curious. "If he can't make it out on his own, with the power at his command, is there anything you can do to help?"

I bit my lower lip so hard it ached and shook my head. Because that was the sad truth, wasn't it? I couldn't help my son. And I hated myself for it.

Oliver pulled me gently toward him and I sagged against his side, his arm sliding around my shoulders. It had been a long time since I had someone to lean on. An equal. Hell, had I ever had someone who felt like they matched me in power and responsibility? I'd used Liam as a resting place, but he'd always been a safe haven, not a partner if I was honest about it. And Quaid's tie to me through the magic that linked us had given me a false sense of perfect. One that I saw as a lie the moment I broke that connection. He, too, had been less than I needed, though I hadn't seen it until later.

Was I lying to myself about Oliver, too? Possibly. Did it matter? His fingers curved, stroked over my skin where they rested on my upper arm, sending a shiver through me. An intimate touch, but not meant that way, I don't think. I wouldn't have allowed anything that wasn't a simple gesture of warmth and support. But it felt good to have him there beside me, to feel the beating of his heart and the pillar of steel within him. I'd never needed anyone else, but it was nice, wasn't it? Knowing I had someone to lean on who didn't see me as anything but just like him.

"Gabriel will be all right," Oliver said with such conviction my breath caught. "He is the Gateway and Creator has his back." I had to agree with him there. But even She didn't seem to have control of the situation. Or did She? Didn't I just assure Oliver everything was as it was supposed to be? Hypocrite, thy name is Sydlynn Thaddea Hayle.

I nodded then, exhaled, saw my breath in the air by the light over the back door. It was dark, the moon out of phase, but the stars hid from me thanks to the light of Wilding Springs diffusing their light. Made me sad, thinking about how much of the Universe was lost, how much was left to go. Time to act and pretend I was actually effectual. "So, shall we pick something we can do something about from our long list of disasters waiting to happen?"

Oliver's arm tightened and he laughed. "I'm all for a prison break."

That was on my mind, too, when Max's mental touch perked me up and drew my attention.

Syd. Fear, held carefully tight and contained, but present and pending. Oliver sat upright immediately, clearly in the loop as Max's concern washed over both of us. *Oliver. Something is happening. I believe the time has come.*

At first I wondered about the dream, kicked myself for not sharing it. Was he having it, too? But Max was already opening up, though as I shed the instant of thought for the veil's hum of fear, it turned out he didn't need to show me, expose where he was. Didn't stop him. The edge of the veil, where the two that were one existed on either side of a border that should never be crossed. No need to see the outward bowing of energy, the bubbling of the barrier. I felt it, the instant it happened, hearing as I endured the pain the cry of the veil at the assault. Both of us did, Oliver's guilt written over his face, writhing in his magic as the two of us sat, staring into each other's eyes in our physical forms, our magic with Max, while the barrier between the Universes split and the Order marched through.

TWENTY-ONE

It took me a moment of utter terror before I realized that wasn't exactly accurate. While the Order was definitely one step closer to our Universe, they weren't quite all the way through. I felt them stop, held back by a thin, vibrating barrier, that odd feeling of time I'd encountered the first moment I'd understood what the line between Universes might be.

So no need to panic, right? Oliver didn't seem to agree.

I have to go. He half stood, hand shaking, his gray eyes wide and full of fear. But I pulled him back down beside me while Max's deep voice echoed my denial with speech.

There is nothing your departure will do now, he sent, quiet and calm despite the initial fear of our contact. *They seem to be stymied inside some kind of bubble of power.*

I saw it clearly through his mental touch, though it

seemed so frail to me, the last barrier between us and them. And while there was no sign of Dark Brother behind them, the space flooded with warriors in shining armor, widening outward, bulging into our Universe like a tumor. Drachmor soared in the space above the towering heads of the Order soldiers, pushing against the last defense we had.

Could it be Gabriel? I hated to ask the question, to lay blame on my son. But his departure into the void might have triggered a weakness. How I had no idea. Clearly, grasping at straws was a favorite pastime of mine.

I highly doubt it, Oliver sent. *More than likely, this is my fault.*

Or mine for going over there in the first place. I fretted, despite knowing we had to go, that the heart needed to be retrieved.

Are you two done searching for someone or something to blame? Humor in Max's voice. Imagine. I spluttered in protest as he went on, Oliver's terror fading to resigned acceptance with the hint of a grin on his face. *Because I can wait if you're not through.*

You, cracking a joke? Okay, the Universe really is in trouble. I sent that with a mental hug and a laugh that shook with the remnants of my fear.

His mind, so dark and quiet lately, flexed with good humor before he retreated from me again. *It seemed appropriate considering your state of mind.*

Thanks for talking me off the ledge. I shook off the last of my panic and drew a deep breath. *So, we still have some time, is that it?*

Apparently. Max observed the influx into the bubble with much more critical objectiveness than I ever could have mustered even in the best of circumstances. *It would seem they are moving ahead with their attempt to penetrate our Universe, but have only achieved partial success.*

The weakness of the veil, I sent. *That has to be the reason they can even breach this far.*

Agreed, Max sent. *So yes, your fault, our fault. Creator's.* He sounded amused again. How could he at a time like this? Made me want to stress giggle despite the weight of the situation. *I'll be sure to bring it up with Her when the statue is complete.*

Oh, I've got a whole heaping pile of stuff to bring up when that happens. Creator better watch out. *In the meantime, is there anything we can do to keep them locked into their Universe?*

My people will stand guard, he sent, now sounding and feeling tired. The drach moved around him, all in full dragon form though I understood why he chose to remain in his human body. No wings. We really had to find a way to correct that.

Another thing for Creator to handle when this was over.

Keep us posted. I hated to leave him, felt like I was abandoning him, but his mind felt distant, as though he were encouraging me to back off. So I did, closing down the connection and drawing a deep, cleansing breath into the cool air of the dark back yard.

Oliver stood, paced into the browning grass, then spun to face me. Light from the back doorway cast long shadows of his tall body, reflected on half of his face, the rest of him in darkness. "I can't just sit on my hands anymore, Syd." It must have felt that way to him, I guess. His fingers ran through blond waves, jaw clenching and unclenching as he swayed on his feet. "I can go to Max, see if I can help?"

I stood, went to him, sent him a wash of calm I really didn't have the right to be in possession of. But did, thanks to the drach lord. "If you go out there," I said, doing my best not to set him off, pulling deep on Mom and Max and everyone in my life who seemed better at this stuff than I was, "your presence could trigger their crossing."

Oliver paled, turned away, both hands in his hair, clutching at his skull before he spun back, arms dropping suddenly while desperate regret passed over his handsome face. "You should have let me die."

"Why?" This wasn't his fault. Max was right to poke at us for our need to place blame.

He shrugged, arms crossing over his chest, hands hugging himself, head down. "I was supposed to die, Syd."

That was news. "According to whom?"

He looked up, met my gaze with his own, gray eyes sparking with light both from the illumination over the back door and his own inner power. "Fate." He swallowed convulsively while I stared at him in stunned silence. "She told me a while ago. I've been ready for it for months now." He dropped his grip on himself and shrugged, wide mouth downturned in sorrow. "I'm a soldier, Syd. A warrior of the Order. I hate who my people are, who I was forced to be when I was with them. This was a way out." He slid his hands into his pockets, shoulders rising as he turned from me again. "A chance to make a difference and change the Universe."

"That's why you volunteered to come with me when I went for Max." He thought he was going to die. "So you did have a death wish." The idiot. I wanted to smack him. And hug him. And maybe kiss him. Then smack him again.

Oliver's grin was grim. "She told me my life would end," he said.

Wait a second. "Repeat exactly what she said." Fate. So tricksy.

Olivier's brows furrowed, eyes meeting mine again as he stopped, hesitated. Groaned. "I heard what I wanted to hear from her, didn't I?"

"Just tell me." Sigh.

"She said you would come." He uncoiled slowly,

strain and tension leaving him while he visibly pondered as he spoke. "That I had to be ready. When you arrived, my job was clear. To protect Doombringer at any cost. Help her return to her own Universe. And that my life as I knew it would end." He shook his head and laughed, weak but there. "That the light would find me." His gray eyes held sadness, but mirth, too. "I thought she was talking about my death. But she meant coming here. And taking on the white sorcery."

I nodded, punched him gently in the arm, my own lips twisting into a smile. "You're supposed to be here," I said. "So stop looming and moping and make yourself useful."

He shivered, rubbed his arms, looked up into the dark sky a moment, a genuine smile on his face before he reached out and embraced me. I found myself pressed to his wide, hard chest, the scent of fabric softener in my nostrils, the pillar of steel inside him softened by his joy.

"Yes, ma'am," he said.

Heat fired between us, the press of his body making my cheeks warm, other parts of me wake and tingle. Oliver released me partially, enough I could look up into his eyes, note the glint of come hither in his eyes, absorb the way he relaxed against me. Natural, like we fit together in ways I'd never experienced before. I held still, breathless, as he bent his head over me, the inevitable calling.

Her power broke us apart, her apologetic cough jerking me free of Oliver's arms, flushing my face even redder than his embrace had done. Trill's own cheeks were pink even in the wash of bright light over the doorway. The only person who didn't seem out of sorts by the whole thing was Oliver. He smirked at me, nodded to Trill like the fact he'd been about to kiss me was no big deal.

I should have been grateful she interrupted, right? Of course I should have. I couldn't afford to get attached to the big lummox. Had more than enough on my plate without emotional complications or letting my hormones get the best of me.

Spoilsport, my demon grumbled.

So why then was I so irritated when Trill shrugged her apology? Couldn't she have waited two more freaking seconds? At least then I would have known what Oliver tasted like.

Groan.

"You know about the Order?" My tone was crisp, I admit it.

Trill nodded, all business while Oliver leaned in closer to me than he really had the right to. I could feel the heat of his body, distracted by his proximity enough it just amped up my irritability.

"I'm not here because of that," she said, the last of her embarrassment falling away to troubled concern. That helped shake me out of the vestiges of my attraction to Oliver and forced me to focus. Yes, good. Disaster was an excellent antidote to lust. "Things aren't happening the way they are meant to," she said. I'd heard that from her before, not so long ago. "Someone is purposely manipulating Fate in this Universe."

TWENTY-TWO

I opened my mouth to offer my supposition as to who that might be when Mom's mental touch jerked me out of this conversation and into another.

Syd. Tense, imminently stressed. I could feel my mother moving, feet hurrying down a hallway, heavy skirt clinging to her legs, silk shirt cold against her skin. She was letting a lot through in her anxiety. I caught flashes of the inner council chamber at Harvard, flares of blue light as Enforcer fire appeared in her periphery while she stormed into the big room, warped in my mind's eye by living through her experience. She spun quickly, too fast, my brain unable to process fully, outside the dark robed shapes appearing in a rush, hearing the screaming of witches as more blue flames licked and burst around them. Enforcers. Whose?

Didn't matter. Mom's mind tightened. *I need you.*

No question, no hesitation. I didn't even answer her, abandoning Trill in the back yard at Wilding Springs, Oliver on my heels, stepping through the veil and into the same council chamber a moment later to the sight of Femke and her Enforcers facing off with my mother.

Oh, no she did *not*.

Mom's mind remained linked with mine, her booming voice echoing in my head first as a mental send then to words as I arrived.

YOU HAVE "no right to be here." Okay, so she was only shouting in my mind. Her tone was much more reasonable on the ground. *Sorry*, Mom sent.

"Council Leaders." I nodded to both of them as if I'd just strolled in after a nice bite of lunch.

Femke snarled at me, her power hitting me hard. Hard enough I knew it wasn't her in control any longer. With Quaid arrested, she'd lost her last bastion of strength against the Black Soul sorcerer inside her. Damn it, I should have sent someone after her, but between Varity's death and Quaid's arrest, not to mention the mess with Gabriel leaving and now the Order's attempt to breach our Universe...

A girl could only juggle so much before a few balls hit the floor.

Case in point.

"This council," Femke said, voice brittle but carrying through her power to every single witch in the North

American territory, "is officially disbanded."

Mom repeated herself, still firm, standing her ground. "You have no right."

"I have the authority of the World Paranormal Council," Femke said. No, not Femke. Konstantin. "With a unanimous vote of all other world witch territories, the North American Council has been deemed invalid and unlawful and will be disbanded immediately."

Syd. I was shocked to find Trill at my side, standing right next to me. Ignoring what was happening before us, focused entirely on me. *If we don't do something, the Order might break through. Fate must be allowed to act autonomously and without interference.*

Wait, what? I shook my head, trying to remember which conversation I was in the middle of. *Can't this wait?* Mom needed me, damn it.

No, it can't. Trill's power prodded me, and I realized then I wasn't the only one—or my son, for that matter— who managed to maintain earth, air, water and spirit magic despite the loss of those elements into the void. Trill had hers, too. I didn't have time to explore what that might mean, not while Femke's magic slammed down over my mother and tried to crush her.

When I lashed out to help, Trill's power stopped me. Stopped Oliver at the same time. I was so shocked I gaped at the young Zornov maji, heart pounding, the whole world going still for a single instant while the

Order soldier continued to fight, grim, determined, his gray eyes locked on my mother.

Syd! Mom's mind reached mine, desperate now. The young North American Council's power fought back against Femke, snarling and furious, but it was no match and I knew it.

Let me go. How? How was Trill so powerful she could stop me, stop both of us? This wasn't right. Stunned, floored, bowled over, I couldn't even muster enough energy to be angry.

We have to go. Now. Trill glanced over her shoulder at Mom, guilt flickering a moment. *They're cheating,* she whispered and I had the impression I wasn't supposed to hear that. *So I cheat, too.* And felt the whip crack of her magic as it reached out, not to stop Femke, but to call for help.

Piers came a moment later, a giant, black tunnel opening right next to my mother, the full force of the new Sorcerers League at his beck and call. He saluted me, Mom gasping for air when he supported her and gave her respite, pushing back against Femke and her Enforcers.

"At your service, North America," he said with a jaunty wave for the WPC leader.

Mom's eyes met mine without judgment though I was hating on myself and Trill and the damned Universe for keeping me away from her. "Our deepest gratitude, Leader Southway." *Go,* she sent, voice level but shaking slightly. *Thank you.*

For nothing. I snarled at Trill as she sliced open the veil and pulled me through with her, Oliver marching behind, leaving Piers and my mother to battle Femke. *This isn't right. I have to go back.*

Not this time, Trill sent. *They will be fine.* Why did she sound like that was a lie? A huge, fat, horrible lie I'd be furious about later. *But if we don't act, it's over.* She stopped, stared into my eyes, her lips thinned out, eyes hooded and dark. *Do you understand? Over.*

I glanced at Oliver. He looked angry, truly angry. For me? At Trill? Didn't matter, I guess. He offered a vague gesture of acceptance, face grim and tight. Shaken by her ability to contain him, as I was. Not that I needed his agreement, but knowing he was willing to listen helped me make my own choice.

The Universe needed me. Creator needed me. I'd promised to trust. I just hadn't expected to have to choose between those I loved and Fate.

Now who was the liar?

I shrugged off my anger at her, forced myself to be a grown up though the big girl panties pinched, didn't they? *Let's go.*

Max seemed shocked to see us, his surprise only lasting a moment, practiced calm back all over again. He nodded to Trill who ignored him, floated past him, staring with hurt and anger at the bubble. I'd seen it through the drach lord's eyes, yes, but there was nothing like hovering in what remained of the veil with a vast, shimmering blister pushing outward toward you, growing by the moment, flooding with the shining, armored forms of your enemies.

I'd been witness to some amazing and terrifying things in my life and knew if I survived what was coming I would again. But as I hung there in the rubber membrane of my Universe and watched the forces of Dark Brother encroach, my heart plummeted to my feet.

So many of them, despite the outflow of their number to the void. And the drachmor, their giant forms flying, slithering their way further and further into my Universe. They, it seemed, remained as large in ranks as the drach, untouched by the disappearances into the darkness between planes. I struggled for breath, for the ability to shunt the enormity of what was before me aside and leap on the task at hand—whatever Trill thought that was— but this was so big, too big. Universal. How could we possibly win against such a foe that seemed so determined to find their way in?

Someone's hand slipped into mine, big fingers tightening over my cold skin. I squeezed back, looked up to see Oliver staring at the foothold of his people with a grim expression that devoured the light in his eyes. So much for staying away, for my empty warning. Him being here did nothing to increase the expansion. That was already happening on its own.

I felt it then, the softening of the barrier and understood where we were.

I know this spot, I sent to Trill.

Yes, she answered without turning around. Anger crackled in her mental voice. *The doorway I left for you to cross over.*

The soft spot in the barrier between Universes. *They weren't supposed to find it?*

No. Lightning sparked. *They weren't.*

Well, that sucked. *I take it this means we're in serious trouble.* So much for trusting Fate.

Trill finally turned, met my eyes. I'd never seen her so angry, so determined. *Fate*, she snarled, and for the first time ever I was afraid of her. Grateful I hadn't done anything to make her so very furious, bad enough I had to hover there and take the blow of her compressed rage while she lashed out with words. *I'll kick her ass.*

Would have made me laugh if the situation wasn't so grim. Felt sorry for Zoe for a brief heartbeat before jumping on the Trillrage gravy train. Why would she betray her own Universe? And how did Trill know what was supposed to happen? That was Zoe's job, right? I wanted to ask the young Zornov just what her role was here but she was already answering me.

I will not let outside forces ruin what we've sacrificed. She chopped one hand through the air. *Their part comes later.*

Poking their noses in now only leads to chaos.

Whatever that meant. *Can you stop them?* Dear elements, what was I asking? Trill? Could she?

She hesitated, anger ebbing as she thought about it. Finally shook her head. Just the fact she contemplated it made me shudder with wonder. She could. But chose not to.

Come.

I followed her, if only to get answers to giant questions that ran through my head like gerbils on drugs. *Where?*

To deal with Zoe Helios, she sent. *And act against our own Fate if I must. To save everything.*

No way was I missing this show.

TWENTY-THREE

It took a lot of convincing to leave Oliver behind. Time I really didn't have. So much I almost caved as Trill waited for me, impatience on her face and a feeling of utter frustration in her power.

You need backup. He loomed over me like always, only this was the first time he'd ever tried to bully me.

Max laughed. Out loud. So not like him. He'd been meandering between total silence and lighthearted boyishness lately. I worried, of course I did. But his amusement felt appropriate.

Syd, he sent directly to Oliver though the drach lord turned to meet my eyes, *needs no one.* I wasn't sure if he meant it as a compliment or not. But how else should it come across? Something dark lurked in Max's gaze, a hurt that had to be linked to his missing wings. Did he blame me? Maybe for saving him, in the end. I winced inwardly, remembering how painful it had been to give up my drach form and I'd only been at it six months. Come to think of it, Max hadn't shown up in his dragon shape since his wing stumps had healed over. Did he wish I'd left him in the other Universe to die?

Oliver didn't back down despite Max's statement. *You're the one who has trust issues when it comes to her.* He didn't seem to care Trill was watching, heard what he sent to me. *And you're going to run off with her alone? Now?* He waved at the expanding bubble. *How about us, then? We need you, Syd.*

You don't get to use guilt on me, soldier, I snapped. *Ever.* Little did he know I was already doing so, which meant his attempt was redundant to the point of ridiculousness. *Tell you what, you explain to the young lady over there why it is you need to come and I'll just wait here.*

He glanced at Trill who shook her head.

Can we go now? She had reverted to the snappish, cranky soul I'd first met. *Alone?* I loved how she stressed that word. *She hardly needs a babysitter. And your power might be required here.* Sounded to me like I wasn't the only one with trust issues.

Should I be worried about him? I threw that at Trill in as tight a question as possible.

I don't know. Her fretting felt vulnerable, unlike her lately. *I just don't, Syd. We have to go. And he'll be in the way.*

I nodded abruptly, decision made. *Sit,* I sent. *Stay.*

Good boy.

Oliver growled at me under his mental breath. But, to his credit, he did as ordered while I followed Trill through the cut she made in the veil.

I feel like I'm letting them down. I didn't mean to confess that to her but from the look on her face, the hurt in her eyes, she agreed with me.

This is going all wrong, she sent. *I need to fix it, Syd. Before it's too late.*

What's your role in all this? Maybe in her present state of mind she'd be willing to let something slip.

I should have known better. Her lips clamped together, eyes shuttering from her open honesty into guarded once again. *We still have some time,* she sent. *The Order needs to find a way to break through the moment that makes up the barrier. But they won't be long at it, I'm afraid. Follow my lead.* She turned away from me, determination written all over her, threading through her power. *And back me up.*

Like she needed my backup from the way she'd been talking. And feeling. She'd stopped both me and Oliver from helping Mom without even breaking a sweat. Still. It was a novelty, wasn't it? Being someone else's bodyguard.

Okay then.

I don't know where I was expecting to step out of the veil, but the chapel in the Sanctuary wasn't it. My sneakers touched down on stone as I absorbed where we were, far under the city of Los Angeles even as Zoe spun from where she stood, speaking to someone blocked by her body, the pair of them at the altar in the darkened stone room.

The moment she turned, a gasp telling me Fate wasn't so up on her advanced warnings these days, my entire body clenched in fury. Because the sudden exposure of Bellanca, the former Light Fate, told me everything I needed to know. Confirmed my fears. Slapped me in the face with betrayal even as the maji woman scowled.

But it was Trill who faced down the ex-Fate, whose power crackled and burned the air, leaving behind a hint of charred ozone in her fury.

"You!" She stormed past Zoe and planted a shove in Bellanca's chest, knocking the woman physically back away from the Helios Fate. Where a magical attack might have been countered or even failed all together, from the shock on Bellanca's face she hadn't been expecting a personal blow. But Trill was on a roll, hitting the blonde again, making Bellanca stagger into the stone surround of the altar and pinning her with a savage growl. The railing cracked with a sharp sound like a bullet firing from a gun, making me jump. "How dare you interfere?"

Bellanca's face twisted, Zoe reaching out for both of them, but I got in the Helios Oracle's way, knowing this was Trill's issue to deal with.

"Mind your own business, child," the former Fate snapped. "Your insignificant toilings are of no matter to more important foresights."

Trill hit her again, though Bellanca seemed shielded against such a blow this time, only swaying slightly though she paled as if Trill's strength was unexpected.

"You have no idea," Trill said, voice now quiet, deep and vibrating with power. Universal power. "Who I am. Or what my purpose is."

Was it wrong I hoped she'd blurt it out so I'd have my answers? Fascinating to stand there and watch the two battle it out with words and magic, to be the one on the outside for once. My heart might have doubted her a time or two—okay, more than that—but in that moment it cheered for Trillia Zornov.

"Let her go." Zoe's own voice shook. She tried to push me out of her way, to go to Bellanca, but I held her back with little effort, absently. She snapped her magic at me only to hit a barrier about as powerful as anything I'd ever raised before. Eyes widening, she shook her head at me. "Not possible. I'm Fate."

"You are," Trill snapped over her shoulder. "And were your path true, nothing would hold you back. So tell me, Zoe Helios. Who do you trust? Creator? Or this fallen soul who means all of us ill?"

Bellanca spluttered while Zoe hesitated beside me. "Don't listen to her," the maji woman said, voice trying for soothing, it sounded like, but abrasive in my ears. "We've talked about this. We both know the end is coming. And you're chosen to see it through."

Zoe tensed beside me, nodded. "Step aside, Trill."

But the Zornov maji barked a laugh, pushed harder against Bellanca, stone crumbling from the pressure. "Is that what you're trying to do?" She sighed, deep and long, heartbreaking as she sagged a moment though her power never relented, not an iota. "You're all fools, every single one of your second race asses. I'll deal with you eventually. When I've fixed this mess you've made."

Okay, hang on a damned second. Trill was talking like she had control over Fate. Over everything. What did that mean, exactly? I didn't get to challenge her, to demand an answer. Not when her mind, now massive in her power, connected with mine.

I can't reach for her, she sent and I shuddered from the vastness of who she'd become. No, who she was becoming. Like my son, I could feel the Universe in her. *But you can.*

Who? She was lucky I was thinking straight enough, had experience acting despite overwhelm and shock, to ask that meager question.

You know who. She hit me with an image, irritation scorching. I veered from Trill but got the message, suddenly afraid and euphoric after contact with so much power.

And reached across the barrier without hesitation, through the thinned out time that was the last thing keeping the Universes apart, to touch the mind of Fate.

Mia answered immediately, with fury, shock. *What are you doing? Don't you realize what's happening right now? That Fate is going to hell and it's your side's fault?*

I do, I sent, teeth clamped against her rage and fear. *But she needs help.* I showed Mia the scene before me, Trill and Bellanca. The battle being waged across Zoe's face. *From what I've been told, if we don't help her, it's all over now.*

Mia's mind settled instantly. *Understood*, she sent. *And now I know why this is happening outside my sight. Let me in.* She shouldered her way past me, past the girls who grumbled and huffed and stepped aside with a prim, *Excuse us, then.*

Zoe registered the change instantly, face settling, calm returning. As if Fate called to Fate and released her from whatever spell her old mentor held her under.

Even as power burst, released, recoiled while Bellanca shouted, "NO!"

TWENTY-FOUR

Magic recoiled like a thrown knife with its edge on fire, the thread tying Bellanca to Zoe snapping with the force of an explosion the instant Mia linked with her alternate Fate. Whatever Bellanca had done to influence the Helios Oracle flew back at her and slammed into her, past Trill who stepped aside to allow the returning energy to carry Bellanca to her knees, to her face.

Zoe staggered forward into my arms and I caught her, feeling Mia detach from me, releasing us from her control. But she didn't return to her own Universe right away, instead solidifying her image and facing down her counterpart while the young Helios Oracle gaped at her in residual shock at her release. My power lunged for Bellanca the moment she tried to rise, but it was too late. I felt it the instant she decided to run, could do nothing to stop her as she dove into the veil and disappeared.

Glared at Trill who let her go, frowning so deeply I relented my own anger. *An order for everything, even the ex-Fate?*

Trill didn't respond.

Idiot, Mia sent, frown on her face. Aimed at Zoe, not me. *You know better than to trust anyone but that which gives us truth.*

Zoe shook her head, one hand pressing to her forehead while I helped her stand upright. *Old ties*, she sent in return, facing down her alternate as her strength and balance returned. *Unexpected. I didn't recognize the hold she had over me. Until it was too late.*

Mia's magic examined Zoe a moment before retreating. *Make sure it doesn't happen again*, she sent, uncompromising, so much so I wanted to defend my friend, shaking beside me. The same friend I'd considered smacking just a moment ago? Yeah, because that was how messed up my head was. Zoe's failure had almost meant our end, sure. But it sounded like it wasn't entirely her fault. I'd rather blame Bellanca. *The timeline has moved up thanks to your mess. Clean it up before we're forced to choose ourselves.*

Zoe blanched, wincing visibly, bright spots on her olive cheeks as she nodded. *I shall.*

Mia softened slightly, one hand raised. *I'll see you soon, sister*, she sent. And vanished.

I released Zoe when she stepped away, stunned half

smile out of place. She had to be dazed, shaken. Tears welled in her eyes but she maintained that little grin that told me she was on the edge of her own fight with guilt and grief. I struggled with my questions. On the one hand, she might be willing to talk in her present state. That had to be the single most frustratingly tantalizing conversation I'd never been a part of. How could they do this to me? Let me witness this meeting, their discussion, and not tell me anything?

On the other, she was vulnerable and a mess.

I'd regret it later. Time for answers now.

I didn't get to drill Zoe after all. From the scowl on Trill's face, the way she shook an index finger in my direction, she knew where my head was. "Don't," she snapped. "Just don't."

I shrugged, angry at last, afraid of her, too, but unwilling to let it stop me. "You brought me."

Trill laughed then, all of her rage running out of her, exposing the terrible fear on her face for a moment. She rubbed at her cheeks with both hands before slumping against the low, stone wall circling the altar, part of it crumbled from her battle with Bellanca. "I had to be saddled with you," she said. "Didn't I? Freaking wild card of Creator." She giggled. "So not fair."

Smartass. "What about Bellanca?" Surely that was a safe question.

"Doesn't matter now," Trill said, exhaling softly while

her face settled into calm. She seemed almost serene compared to the last few minutes. "Now that what's done is done, I had to let her go. She has a part to play later, thanks to how things have unfolded. A fate I'd hoped to avoid." Trill seemed saddened by that, but went on. "At least for now she's done messing with our Fate."

Zoe choked on a soft sob, hugged herself. "I can't believe I let this happen." Her dark eyes met mine, full of guilt. "How bad?"

"Bad," I said. "The Order. The drachmor." I showed her as I finished. "They're almost through."

Her hands flew to her face, covered her gaping mouth. Tears trickled down her cheeks, her regret a physical thing that bumped against me in its need to flee and hide. "My fault."

Max's earlier joking came back to me. "Blame," I said, hugging her so she wouldn't run. "My favorite."

She gasped a soft laugh but embraced me back. Accepted my support, my offer of understanding. Allowed it to comfort her, to soften the blow of what I'd told her. She shivered until she was still and then released me. Turned and threw herself at Trill who had come quietly to join us. "I'm so sorry."

"Me, too," Trill whispered. "I should have watched you more carefully."

Zoe hiccupped, wiped at her wet cheeks. "Well," she said, trying a smile on for size, a real one to replace the damaged little grin. "Creator seemed to have made a mistake or two along the way. We're a bit of a disaster, aren't we?"

I offered a grin. "Speak for yourselves," I said. "Been down this road enough, I'm the definition of put together, thanks."

They both laughed. Should probably have been offended. Wasn't. Yeah.

"So now what?" I hated to break up the party but if they were worried, I was worried. All along I'd been working on the supposition this was Fate, that Creator knew what She was doing. If that wasn't the case... how come the other side always got to look like they were the only ones who knew what they were doing while we stumbled around and felt inadequate?

"Things are happening far too quickly," Trill said, biting at her lower lip.

Zoe nodded, voice quavering. "I thought I needed to do what she said," she told us. "Because the path wasn't clear. The future so dim, so dark." She shook her head. "Even free of her, I still can't see the way ahead. Everything is jumbled together."

Trill shrugged. "She must have muddied the waters to make you believe she was telling you the truth through the connection you shared. And, in influencing you, created a true path divergence."

Well, that sucked. Smart. Brilliant, really. Whatever

her game plan, I had to hand it to Bellanca—she'd managed to fool Fate and circumvent Creator. But what was she after? The destruction of the Universe? Was Bellanca that short sighted? Whatever. Didn't matter now, according to Trill. Not when our advantage of seeing the future was gone with Zoe's foresight.

I nodded sagely with both of them before looking up, like I was part of their inner circle or something, not held outside being in the know. Faker. And found them looking at me. Waiting. With expectation, patience. Like I was supposed to say something. Do something.

Wait, outside them, okay. But the one with the answers instead of the other way around?

I laughed again, stomach heaving slightly in anxiety and hysterical giddiness. "Tell me the two of you aren't waiting for me to launch into some brilliant speech that leads you to the answer?" Because that would be terrifying and make me throw up right then and there if it wasn't so damned funny.

Trill's smile hurt because it was so young and vulnerable. "Syd," she said. Stopped. Drew a breath. "This is bad. I'm sorry, it's really bad." She choked. "Universe ending bad."

Zoe's turn to chew her lower lip red. "Bellanca's agenda just put us all at the brink, both Universes."

"That agenda being?" So it did matter then? I looked back and forth between them, but it was Trill who shook her head, tight and tense.

"Later," she said. "The point is we've lost control of what should have been an orderly process." The Universe falling apart was orderly? If she said so. "Now... it could end in disaster." Could. Sounded like "would" more than its counterpart.

"Or success." Zoe's attempt at optimism wasn't making me feel all that confident.

"Where's Gabriel?" Sudden fear struck me a blow. I'd not worried about him—well, not much, or more than usual—due to my faith in Creator. But now? Did Trill's estimation of bad include bigger risk to my son than I'd first guessed? "Is he okay?" Panic clutched my chest, seized control of my heartbeat.

Trill nodded, waved one hand at me like I was panicking over nothing. "He's fine," she said as if my terror wasn't warranted or even something that should be on the table. Which didn't make me feel better, actually. Because I knew what that meant. He was as gigantic as I thought he was.

I'd lost my little boy to the Gateway. And I'd be damned if I was going to let these two leave me in the dark any longer.

Planting my feet, crossing my arms over my chest, I hit them both with a smack of magic and dug in my heels. "You want to fix this?" I prodded them both again. "You tell me what the hell is going on. Once and for all."

The fact they didn't argue hammered the final nail in that particular coffin. Because if they were prepared to fill me in, things were really up the creek with a hole in our boat. Leaking planes into the void and taking our paddles with them.

TWENTY-FIVE

"The maji." It was Zoe who spoke first before stopping herself, olive skin turning red as she nodded to Trill and sighed. "Bellanca and Thanos know where they are."

Grim, irritated all over again, Trill tossed her hands. "There's nothing we can do about that now," she said, like they'd had this conversation before. Well, I hadn't. "You know that. Stay on track."

"What about the maji?" They'd disappeared from Center and Core, gone their own way from what I understood. At first, I'd thought they'd vanished with the other races who went with the elemental magicks. But according to the ex-Fates they weren't in the void after all, were nowhere to be found.

They had to be somewhere. So where?

"I'm telling you," Trill said, "they don't matter."

Impatience took her words a moment and she tsked past her irritation before speaking again. "Now that we've removed their influence we can get back to what's important." She shot Zoe a *don't mess with me* look. I knew it because I'd used one like it in the past. Was the queen of it, as far as I was concerned. Didn't hold a candle to Trill, it turned out. "We have to focus."

Zoe sighed, returned her attention to me. Now I was freaked out. All along I thought it was Fate pulling the strings. To find out Trill was her boss... or, at least, that's how things came across. Who exactly was the young Zornov? *What* was she? And did I really want to know?

"The second race remains the only wild card in all of our planning," Fate admitted at last though Trill scowled at her admission. "Syd's figured out that much on her own," she said directly to the unhappy maji. Trill shrugged it off and looked away. "They've taken themselves out of play at this point. So Trill is right about one thing. As long as the maji stay away, they aren't our problem right now." In other words they would be shortly. Just not at the moment. Gotcha. Still hated not having all the answers, though.

"What if Bellanca returns?" Did I have to worry Zoe might fall under her influence again? And where was the ex-Fate's brother in all this? I hadn't seen Thanos here, at least. Didn't mean I could trust him or anything, but he scored for not trying to manipulate the new Fate. Or was he in a more subtle way we had yet to detect?

"You already know what's coming," Zoe said, sadness in her voice. "You spoke it not so long ago, Syd. Woke the possibility. And though the future is fuzzy to me right now, murky thanks to the interference of my predecessor, the end *is* coming."

Right. The end of everything. I'd asked about the dark maji, the war Zeon wanted to wage against Gabriel, calling him evil, an abomination. Both Bellanca and Thanos reacted badly to that line of questioning. Was it really almost eight months ago? So short a time, a distance that felt like forever. Though, I refused to add that particular guilt to my already overloaded burden. If the end was coming it was going to happen no matter what I did or said. At least, that's what I told myself as I shook off the niggling worry Doombringer was going to be my life's story.

"If we're done here," I said, "I have my mother to worry about." That guilt I owned 100%, even more so when I felt her wriggling in the background, Piers beside her, and knew without a doubt their situation was much more dire than this one.

Trill went silent, brooding as Zoe nodded, looking sad.

"If you get the chance," she said, "tell Piers…"

I didn't wait to find out if she was going to finish her request. "I'll tell him." *Mom.* I sent that directly to her as I spun and returned into the veil, leaving Fate and whoever Trill was behind to whisper their secrets to each other. Bitter much? *I'm on my way.*

You'd better hurry, Mom sent in a tight, anxious burst of magic. *If you want Harvard to stay standing.*

I winced, opening the way into the council chamber past a giant wave of power trying to keep me out. Not just Femke's, but the black and white ripple of Piers and the furious young magic Mom commanded. Way worse than I expected. The room had filled with smoke, the shouts of Enforcers and bursts of energy exploding over and over as war raged. All-out war. And I could feel it spreading over the whole plane, sorcerer taking on witch.

Like a powder line of explosive had been lit with that assault on Mom's territory, it roared outward in a vast network of webbed magic, igniting fires as it went. What the hell? I felt it, felt the disintegration of loyalties, the surge of anger and hate, the sparks turned to raging infernos that swept out of magical hands and began to assault normals.

Panic bit deep, choked off my air. I had to stop this. Had to save them. My white sorcery sliced through all resistance and I strode forward into the middle of a battle.

Tried to, that is. Took that step forward, anticipated beating sense into all of them, to find a way to stop what felt like a snowball of hell descending on my plane, only to be bounced back. No, pulled back, the veil sealing shut on my mother's startled face.

Syd!

I spun with a snarl on Trill who stood behind me in the echoing quiet of the Sanctuary chapel, her power cutting me off from Mom, from Piers. The burning of my adrenaline drove me close to madness, my need to act spinning inside me in a vast, devouring tornado. Powerful or not, the boss or not, she would regret this just as soon as I was able to focus past my shock and rage. "What the hell are you doing?"

It was Zoe who answered, tears trickling down her cheeks, hands held out to me. "I see now," she whispered. "You can't. I'm so sorry." She hid her face under shaking fingers, shoulders trembling as they curved forward. "This wasn't supposed to happen, but now it is. Fate has decided. Balance has to be restored."

"How are the deaths of countless sorcerers and witches supposed to bring *balance?*" I drove the question into both of them with a lance of magic, wanting to hurt them, my terror for the ones I loved building by the second. "Of normals caught up in what's happening out there?" Shaylee cried out in my head as the earth itself protested, the city above us catching the fire of power that blazed bright, so hot it would burn itself out long before anyone could stop it.

Dear elements. There would be no survivors if

someone didn't intervene.

"Creator knows," Trill said, blunt. Cold.

Oh, *hell* no. I slammed into her, ready to take her on, but she remained immovable, solid and far more powerful than I'd ever imagined she could be. Again I hit her, desperate to shake loose, to find a way to free myself. I'd been here before, in this situation, with Max. Long ago, the day Liam died. I'd fought with every single ounce of strength in me to save my husband and failed. No way was I losing again.

No. Way.

But she held fast, Zoe's power tied to Trill's. The two of them, betrayers both. They couldn't block out the full impact of their refusal to act, couldn't protect me completely from the devastation happening above ground. Enough reached me I knew even normals were now being devoured in multitudes in the firefight. In moments, the world, the entire plane, would burn. Dying. For what?

"Syd." Trill swallowed, even she looking pale and a little green around the edges as though feeling the world fall apart hit her harder than she'd expected. "This is the first plane. This place." The truth of that made sense to me, despite my terror and shaking fury. "It was meant to fall last, when the time came. But if we're going to win it has to fall now."

"I don't understand." Maybe I never would. Even if

the explanation was flawless.

Trill sagged again, the weight of the death of the plane above on her shoulders, visible like a shadow pushing her down. "It's too big for you to understand," she said. "Maybe, when this is over. If it goes the way we need it to. Ask me then. But for now, for better or worse, our time is up. We have to let this go." She shook her head. "Let them go."

I gaped at her, power failing me, shock knocking the fight out of me. "Just let them die?" My mouth flooded with saliva, stomach churning. "How can we just let them die?"

Trill didn't answer. She didn't have to. Trust in Creator was all over her, inside her, pushed at me like some kind of drug. I couldn't accept it, couldn't swallow that bitter pill. This would break me, finally.

They thought the destruction of the Universe was bad. For me, losing the ones I loved above to war and death while I was forced to stand aside and let it happen? That was my end of everything.

I'd lost my will to fight, but Trill held on even as the battle waged above and grew in intensity. How long did we stand there as the plane's power burst outward and spread to every corner, drawing in all of the magic it could reach? I had no idea my world was such a tinderbox of insanity, that the act of attack from Femke on my mother would set off this chain reaction of destruction so complete it took a mere matter of minutes for the entire plane to catch the disease of hate that drove the magical races left behind to fall on each other with murder on their minds.

Only one thing could distract me from the destruction of the ones I loved. Only one voice could reach me now. And that voice, so precious, did the job the instant Gabriel's desperate plea reached me.

Mom! I need you!

And, with that cry, nothing else mattered.

TWENTY-SIX

I grasped for my son, caught the faintest thread of his mind, even as Oliver found me across the veil, latched onto me, his magic feeding mine. How did he know I needed him?

We have to help him. Zoe and Trill were at my side, hands taking mine on either side, their massive magicks joining the fray as I felt the push of the drach behind Max who joined with Oliver. So Gabriel's cry for help hadn't just reached me, then. All was forgotten, the dying world above, the Universe itself shuddering while the flames of war spread out into what remained and devoured entire planes. Didn't matter, I understood that now. Trill's assurance made sense at last.

Only Gabriel mattered.

With tears standing in my eyes as I leaped out of my body and threw my consciousness toward the boy who was the Gateway, I sent every soul still able to help all love and thanks I could muster at their willingness to abandon their own needs and save my son.

Sure, they had reasons beyond the fact he was the only one who could retrieve the last pieces of Creator, that he was the Gateway to the Universe. But he was my kid and the final remains of my long, lost Liam and I couldn't help but be grateful they were there to back me up when he needed me.

Including the remains of Max wrapped around my wrist, that dark ribbon calling out on its own, the flickering, flying bands of colored light that were the souls of the drach that had become attached to my son. Though they wandered off on occasion, it wasn't uncommon to see them hover over him as he slept and the instant they appeared beside me on the cusp of the void and the veil I threw a command at them.

Save him.

They didn't pause, stringing together in a line of magic that flared as their tips touched and connected, forming a rope of light I followed without hesitation into the darkness. Other Universe Max quivered on my wrist but didn't falter, as steadfast as ever while I screamed my son's name into the black.

GABRIEL!

There, he was there and coming closer, painfully slowly. So much so I feared we weren't strong enough, that we never would be. My magic drained from me in a gush, hemorrhaging into the black while the drach ribbons flickered and went out one at a time. I had no time to consider what that meant, if they were alive or dead or simply drained of power, not when Fate from the Dark Universe added her magic through my physical touch with Zoe.

This must not be, she sent, Mia's mind as vast as the Helios girl's. *Fate must be allowed to decide the end and no other.*

Agreed, Zoe sent. And pushed.

I hope you don't expect me to be on your side after this. That wry whisper in my mind made me gasp and want to weep as Mia let me go. No malice in her words or tone, the kindness of her warning just making things worse. My need to believe in an enemy only went so far. And as I grasped for Gabriel, felt the beginning stirrings of a Gateway forming, I sent her love.

Because she was right, of course. This wasn't bad guys against good guys, though those existed in my mind yet. This was a force of nature that had to be completed or we'd all be destroyed.

I spun and flew for the veil, out of the sucking darkness, the girls pouring their hearts and souls into our escape. It was my vampire who grasped onto the faded ribbons and drew them with us, the sucking sound of our return to the remains of the Universe turning my stomach. When I slammed back into my body I found myself in the veil for real, Fate and Trill still with me, the air flooded with drach, Oliver shining across from me, barely visible as a Gateway formed between us and my son tumbled out into my arms.

And not alone, not without victory. His head lolled backward, hazel eyes catching mine as he smiled weakly, the two eyes of Creator clutched in his hands.

Mom, he whispered in my mind. And passed out.

Maybe I should have taken him to the Stronghold underchamber then and there, but instead habit ruled me. I found myself, a few seconds later, lowering his limp form onto his bed in Wilding Springs, Max and Oliver standing guard at the foot, Trill at my side, Zoe by the door. Sass quickly leaped to the pillow, snuggling his silver Persian body against my son and began to purr, his healing energy washing over Gabriel while I sagged with relief, staring at the washed out, wasted ribbons that lay across my son's chest.

My magic touched them, weary and worn, and found them alive. I wept then, wordlessly, soundlessly, hands at my sides, shoulders shaking for the brave souls and their survival. For our survival while the world around my small town rocked with the battle that waged on and on forever.

Outside his bedroom window, pushing against a dome of power I'd created, the night sky burned.

"What happened?" Oliver shook, though from nerves

or the need to act or real fear I had no idea. I looked up and met his eyes, shrugged, unable to say a word.

"The worst case scenario," Zoe said, sounding sad. "My fault."

Trill waved her off, irritated again. Seemed to be her favorite these days. "No one but Bellanca to blame. And the damned maji."

"Where is everyone?" That from Sass. So he'd not been here when the fight broke out? I couldn't feel Gram or the coven, not directly. There was too much power being expended, burned up. I needed to worry and couldn't. Only Gabriel mattered. Because only he could fix it.

I hoped.

Max flinched. "The Universe dies."

Trill nodded in answer but didn't take her eyes from me. "We have to wake him. He needs to finish this, Syd."

I wiped at the snot running down my upper lip, at my wet cheeks and burning eyes, hitching my breath a few times before gaining control of my vocal chords. "Not yet."

"Yes, yet." She strode forward. When Oliver tried to block her, frowning and protective, bless him, she hit him with power hard enough he staggered aside, shock on his face. "Now. Before it's too late." She wrung her hands in front of her, lips turned sharply downward, tightness creasing the corners of her dark eyes. "Can't you feel them?"

I could, now that she mentioned it. The Order. The drachmor. Dark Brother behind them. The bubble had expanded to a hair's thinness, ready to burst. And I knew, then, there was no choice.

Now it was.

The bed creaked faintly as I sat next to my son and stroked his brow, kissed his cheek. "Gabriel." He didn't wake, didn't stir. Faint fear woke, distant and cringing, like I'd forgotten how to feel and was only just excavating emotion again. I felt so dull, so empty. "Sweets." I pushed power into him, sensed nothing, not a stirring or a moment of awareness. Just quiet, deathly quiet. He breathed, yes. His narrow boy's chest rose and fell, cheeks faintly pink, blood pumping through his veins. But his mind was empty.

I looked up, dread and far off grief choking me a moment. "He won't wake."

Trill joined me while Max stirred and I felt them, the Order, felt the instant of breach. Not a huge hole, just a pinprick, but it wouldn't take them long now to make a way big enough for them to enter.

I couldn't bring myself to care. Not while the boy on the bed didn't respond. Might never again. Was this it, then? The real end? Without him we were lost.

"Gabriel." Trill's power pushed on my son, shook the bed. But even her massive might did nothing to draw him to the surface. A horrible fear he'd never return, that our only hope to fix this—or end it, if that was Fate—crumpled me into a little ball of misery as she tried again and again.

I couldn't watch, couldn't be part of my son's loss. I stood, crossed the room to the door. And only then realized he'd left me, was retreating down the steps, his tall, broad shouldered form disappearing into the gloom of the first floor. I followed Oliver on impulse, heartbroken over Gabriel and now this retreat. Finally caught up to him as I descended the stairs to the basement to find him standing in front of the pentagram on the concrete.

He touched the stand of armor he'd left there, shed when he'd made a life for himself here, however brief. Magic liquefied the metal, turned it to a living thing. I watched it flow from the wooden cradle he'd made for it, dully acknowledged the way it curled itself around his body as if with a soul of its own, morphing the handsome man I'd grown to care about into a soldier of my enemy.

Oliver turned, his helmet under one arm, the veil open at his side to meet my eyes with his own sad gaze. "I have to go," he said. Shuddered when the hole his people made grew to the size of an apple. We both felt it, tied to it, to each other, too. "Before it's too late."

"You're going back to them." Such betrayal. I'd privately expected it and yet hoped it would never happen. But he was one of them, no matter how much I wished otherwise. A soldier of the Order, of Dark Brother no matter his bloodline or desires to be someone else. And my feelings for him—admitted or not—would do nothing to hold him here.

He flinched like I'd hit him. "You doubt me," he said, as if I'd dealt him a deathly blow and not the other way around. "How I wish I could convince you otherwise. But I'm useless to you here, now, Syd. I have only one choice."

"Run to them then," I said, bitterness bursting out of me, feeding my anger. Fed by terror my loved ones were gone, I was alone. Only fire burned in the power that had once been my family and friends. The world died outside the shields I'd built to protect this town I called home. "Go back to that life, you coward. They won't win. You won't." Fierce, fiery, furious. "I'll kill you myself."

He lunged for me, dropping his helmet as he did, the sound of it ringing on the concrete startling me. Allowing him the time he needed to envelop me in his arms, for his lips to descend and cover my mouth.

I kissed him back, just as fierce, just as fiery, just as furious. And he devoured me in return, the heat of his body coming through the metal that housed him, his magic softening it though he crushed me as if he'd never let me go.

When our lips parted, when he drew away, the first to

do so, my hunger needing him more than I'd ever needed anyone before, he panted over me, desperate and sad. "If you believe I'm betraying you," he said, "I really do have to go."

"You'll give them what they need to defeat us." White sorcery burned between us, proof of my words.

Oliver shook his head, blond hair wisping over my cheek. "I'm going to go use my power to seal the breach," he said. "And buy you time. You idiot." He kissed me again, let me go so suddenly I staggered back from him, hurting and crying all over again. "I thought I'd have to die for you once, Syd. For a brief respite I had the hope I was wrong. Now?" He shrugged, armor gleaming with power. "Maybe my timing was just off."

The bubble's hole widened as Oliver's head turned toward the hole in the veil. It was visible on the other side, the ranks of Order soldiers shining, drachmor soaring. And Dark Brother's heavy presence pushing behind them all. I shuddered, grateful to be on this side of the gap, knowing it wouldn't matter shortly, that once He crossed it would all be done and gone. What remained, however little that was.

Oliver shivered then met my eyes one last time, smiling at me. A real smile despite the fear lurking in his gaze, his people a backdrop in the veil beside him. "I love you," he said, joy in it. "I never knew there was such a thing until I saw you for the first time. Standing there so defiant, full of life despite everything that happened. You're so brave and beautiful and I have to save you if I can. *My* fate."

I had to stop him, couldn't let him go to his death, too. But a small hand slid into mine, Gabriel's arrival at my side turning my attention as the Gateway lifted his free hand and waved with grave acceptance at the Order soldier.

"This is why you're here," my son said. "We'll see you on the other side."

Magic retrieved Oliver's helmet and, with a salute of his own, he slipped it into place. I didn't get to tell him how I felt, wasn't sure I knew, really. In a blink he was gone, stepped through the gash in the veil to face his people alone, one brave soldier against a sea of darkness.

It sealed shut behind him. I held my breath as the hole in the barrier grew, exhaling outward at Oliver's arrival, my heart and mind latched onto him, seeing him begin to glow, his armor carrying white light outward as he shone brighter and brighter, a star in the black.

The gap between Universes shivered. Growled.

Shrank. And held.

Oliver. Be safe.

"Mom." I looked down at my son who looked back with the Universe in his eyes.

"They're dying," I whispered.

"They're dead." He shrugged like it didn't matter

anymore. I was so tired of that phrase. "Unless we act. It's time."

To end everything once and for all? Nothing else to do, I guess. Dull and shaken, I nodded and followed him through the Gateway and to the Stronghold for the last time.

TWENTY-SEVEN

We weren't alone for long as we stepped out into the underchamber, Max and Mabel joining us, Sass in human form, Jiao beside him. Trill and Zoe weren't in evidence, but I couldn't think of them now. Not when the ground underfoot shook so badly I fell to my knees next to Gabriel.

My son didn't waver despite the earth's protests, seemingly untouched by the destructive force heaving beneath us. His hands rose into the air, releasing me, the eyes of Creator appearing in his grasp a moment later as the ribbons of drach power sprang into being, floating around him with agitated expectation. The black strip of the drach soul on my own wrist tightened, sighed. Did he know what was coming? I wish he'd fill me in because I didn't. Not really. Had no clue what to expect while

Gabriel strode to the statue and climbed into Her lap one last time. It seemed to take forever and yet happened so fast. He stood on tiptoe on Her thighs, the eyes in his hands. With one motion as though he'd practiced it, he pressed firmly into the sockets with both gray, stone orbs, completing Her physical form at long last.

And the Stronghold protested as never before. Another shaking so violent the ground beneath me cracked in a series of explosions sending shards of rock upward and outward, projectiles that surely would have killed anyone unguarded by magic. At least I was ready this time, braced myself with power and my spread legs, knees bent to absorb the shock. Who was I kidding? No amount of preparation readied me for the massive denial of the very bedrock at the recreation of what She had once worn as Her body.

At the same moment the Universe vibrated its fury at such audacity. The bubble holding back Dark Brother and his forces flexed outward in a rush of hunger. But the hole in it, the puncture that was their way through didn't expand. I coughed out dust, knowing then Oliver was doing his part. Terror for him leaped into my chest and strangled me, but I resisted reaching for him again, knew there was nothing I could do, that trying to help would only distract me, distract him. But he was alone out there, on the edge of the Universe, fighting his own people to give us the time to destroy everything. How could I have let him go? I wanted to go to him, to protect him and give him strength, to send him power or do something, anything. But my son was here. My child, the Gateway, and I put him firmly first while remorse and guilt took the place of my worry for Oliver.

Compelled to remain. Waiting as the chamber finished its shaking, stilling into sudden, dead silence.

Even as the veil collapsed completely into the void.

I felt it go with little surprise. This was the point, right? I wept at its death cries, let it fail, nothing I could do to help. Doombringer for real. And waited to die, too.

But nothing happened. The only death was in the air, still and empty, echoing. Dust motes hung in my lungs, made my mouth pasty with grit. But I lived. Didn't I? I was pretty sure. Didn't feel changed, at any rate.

This couldn't be right. My battered mind protested survival in the face of all that had gone before. We should have been dead or crushed or powerless, shouldn't we? Had to be. No way we could stay here, alone. Just the few of us who stared in silence at my son on the lap of Creator's completed statue. The sucking sound the void made, the shrieking final cry of the veil as it crumbled and disappeared, devoured by the black. I heard Oliver's distant shout of defiance, felt his love, embraced it and let it go. Lived the bursting of the bubble too late. But even they, the dark ones, were gone into the black that ate everything with indiscriminate hunger.

Gone. Ethie, my darling girl, lost to me. Mom, Dad, Gram, the coven. Charlotte. Piers and Quaid and the beautiful little twins who hadn't stood a chance. Born into an ending not of their making. My sister's final cry reached me, demon magic burning out in the depths of the aching darkness, elemental fire magic the last to go. My own demon huddled inside me, safe in the embrace of the rest of us, as though the disappearing power didn't even know she was there. I didn't have time to react, to feel even as everyone and everything I knew—those that survived the fires and those that didn't—vanished without a trace. Leaving us behind. Only us.

And then I realized we were, in fact, still here. Hovering in the place that had been the Universe. Outside, for the moment. Intact. This plane, this place that had been the home of Creator's physical form for all eternity was all that remained of anything.

Freaky and surreal. I couldn't comprehend, mind staggering drunkenly from the truth.

I'm here, the Stronghold sent, quiet, contemplative. As though he were surprised to find it so. So was I.

"Why?" Did I speak out loud? Likely. They looked to me, Sass and Jiao, Max and Mabel. Gabriel, even, with stars overtaking his hazel eyes.

Max grunted softly, nodded. "Are we here?"

"Still?" Sass finished the question, disjoined as it was.

Gabriel sighed, remained perched on Creator's lap.

More tears threatened as I absorbed my losses. Karyn, Femke, Sage. Simon. All of them gone. But no, this happened too fast, so fast. It couldn't be real.

Doombringer, my mind whispered.

When Gabriel didn't speak, I reached out, just in case. Surely someone else made it, we weren't alone out here, were we? But there was nothing, no veil, no network of planes and people and magic. Only this single place, this world gone quiet again where once it had teemed with new life. As if the entirety of creation held its breath and waited for something.

But what?

I felt her then, Mia Dumont, the Fate on the other side. She was still there, so something of the Dark Universe remained, too. Comforting? Not really. I caught myself moving forward without thinking about it, needing suddenly to walk, to pace, to do something, anything, instead of standing still in the silence and the loneliness.

"We're still here," I said as I passed Max and Mabel, reached Sass. Touched his cheek, met Jiao's dark eyes, before turning and looking up at Gabriel. "Why are we still here?"

My son sadness made the last bits and pieces of my heart shatter into slivers of loss. "Because," he whispered in voice that carried anyway. "It's not done."

But all the pieces were returned... no, wait. One remained, didn't it? "The soul," I said, stunned and shaken. "We failed, then." Defeat tasted like ashes in my mouth, bitter but tasteless. We'd never identified it, figured out what it meant, what the soul of Creator could be. The other pieces, so obvious, physical in their makeup. But what made a soul?

The ribbon on my wrist twitched while Gabriel's face twisted as he looked away. "No, Mom," he said. "We didn't." We didn't? My mind couldn't help repeating his words. "The soul is here." Where? "I'm just..." his hesitation fired my fear all over again. What was he hiding? "I can't wait any longer. But it's a big thing. Bigger than I expected, even though I knew it was coming. And I don't know if I can do it."

"Do what?" I stumbled toward him, felt power hold me back like a gentle embrace that none the less held me away, kept my distance from the statue and the kid I loved with all my heart perched in Her lap. "Gabriel, what do you have to do?"

He met my eyes again, his own color back, the beloved hazel glinting with green. He smiled at me, that smile that was his father and him and me all rolled into one. I tried to go to him again, wanting to hug him to me and keep him from whatever was hurting him so much. But the power held me still and, as he raised his hand and waved, I knew.

Knew. Like a mother knows when her child is going to leave her.

And tried to scream, to fight off what held still, contained, away from him. Exactly as Max had done the day Liam died. But not Max this time.

No. This time it was Creator Herself who wouldn't let me go.

"I love you," my son said. "And I always will. But Mom, I have to do this. We both know Fate isn't to be denied."

No. Please. Not my son.

His body sagged, his little face falling forward, chin on his chest as his soul pulled free and hovered over him. The soul of Creator. The Gateway. One and the same.

Gabriel's spirit sank into the stone, leaving the slumped and empty physical body behind.

An instant to grieve. To lunge for his limp body, suddenly free again. To clutch it to me, release the sob of absolute loss that was the death of my child.

No time for more, though Creator granted me that much, in the end. But the time of such an outpouring was gone. It wasn't enough, would never be, such a blow. Still, I had no choice—the story of my entire existence—when darkness leaped forward and swallowed us whole.

I welcomed it, his warm, empty body against me. And hoped I'd never surface from its depths again.

TWENTY-EIGHT

Quiet. Empty stillness. Calm.

I opened my eyes to the feeling of nothing, the sky overhead pale blue. Not the usual bright, endless blue I was used to. This sky seemed washed out, a ghost of itself, even the small, puffy clouds that drifted overhead faintly transparent.

It took me a minute to process where I was, the feeling of grass under my hands, my head, the warmth of the ground, uneven in places. Emotion, too, was washed like an echo of what used to be. The faint scents of summer, though as pastel as the rest of the world seemed. When I sat up it was slowly, on the edge of confusion as I tried to understand where I was. Why I was.

The backyard. Of course. Wilding Springs. But why of course? My house stood twenty feet away, looking normal, ordinary. Except the white paint appeared washed with gray, the big trees surrounding it dull and their leaves without the depth of luster to their normal green canopy. The air was heavy, still, not a breeze ruffling the branches overhead. Dead quiet, perfectly calm.

A dream? No, not a dream. Too real for that. I gained my feet, face scrunching almost painfully as I frowned into my memories and tried to figure out what happened.

And gasped a faint, painful breath at the sight that wavered before me. Mom. But not Mom, not really. She'd lost her reality, her opaqueness, the see through tone of her skin drawing gooseflesh to the surface. When she faded out of view I hugged myself, only to turn and find Piers standing next to me, staring with empty, gray eyes across the yard before he, too, vanished.

What was this? They came in waves then, witches and demons and drach, races I'd never seen before, washing past me as if they weren't real, mere ghosts of themselves. Some spoke, but their silence was utter and when I tried once to touch one of them I fell back with a shudder at the coldness of their forms.

"I don't understand." I whispered into the dull air, words falling dead to the ground, my voice not carrying past my own lips. But, as I turned and watched them flicker into life and then disappear again, I began to. "The void." Weird to talk to myself, and yet there was no one else who could hear me. "This is the void."

"Yes." I spun with a squeak, found a familiar form watching me from the back door, his smile kind, his blue eyes sparkling with welcome. I rushed to him, needing another soul more desperately than ever and fell into Sebastian DeWinter's arms.

He embraced me close and tight, whispering things into my ear I will never remember but that warmed my frozen heart enough I unwound from the surreal depth of my detachment and was able to draw real breath, to engage and process, to become Syd again. When he released me, I kissed his cheek and touched his hair, so happy to see him again.

"Syd." Alison appeared at his side and I hugged her, too, her body warm against me.

"We've been waiting for you," Sunny said.

More hugs, for her and Uncle Frank. "You survived." I choked on a sob. "You really did."

Sebastian shrugged. "If this is surviving," he said, sad suddenly. "But it's not over yet, Syd."

It wasn't? I wiped at my tears, instant happiness lighting me up. "I can do something, then? To fix this?" Hope, you old rascal.

"Come," Sebastian said, taking my hand. "Let us show you."

How did we begin in my back yard and end up an instant after he spoke in a wooded glade on the outskirts of Wilding Springs? The old coven site. Only it was far larger than I remembered, vast, stretching out like someone took the edge of reality and turned it into a rubber band. The edges warped, the interior containing walls of vampires behind me where I stood with Sebastain and Alison, Sunny and Uncle Frank. The drach were with us, mostly in human form, though some of their dragon shapes flickered to life and back again. And, on the other side of the pentagram in the earth that the me of before knew no longer resided there were the ranks of the Order, the drachmor wheeling overhead.

"I don't understand." Would I ever? Was it my job to comprehend? Creator loved keeping me in the dark. And now I was in the dark quite literally.

Moa came to my side, her small, bent body still appearing mummified, pinpoint black eyes shining beads in her wrinkled face. But her voice was as young and untouched by time as ever when she spoke.

"Creator did Her best," she said. "And went one better." Her small hand gestured and I looked at the Order without fear. Oliver stood next to his mother. Commander Opal didn't move, none of them did, and as I observed the drachmor I realized they hung, suspended and silent, in the quiet air.

"Are we to fight, then?" It would be a shame that it came to this because of the meddling of the maji. Because I wasn't able to do my job. Doombringer.

"No," Sebastian said. "That's not your Fate, Syd."

I think I'm beginning to see where this is going. My vampire's awe made me pause and listen. *We're the Order, are we not?*

Sebastian's smile was as dear as I remembered. "One better," he said.

Evolution. I was beginning to grasp the pieces. "They are," I said. Found words didn't come to me, the ones I needed to explain what I was thinking. My brain just didn't want to fire fast enough. "They were made as they are." That was a bit better. Oliver's confession his people hadn't evolved past their original creation seemed relevant now.

Sebastian touched my cheek with gentle fingers. "Yes, Syd," he said. "The Order was created and that is where their power remained." For centuries and centuries and centuries. "The drachmor recruitment by Dark Brother was an attempt by Creator's sibling to augment his people. But it failed."

Because Dark Brother wasn't about evolution, was he? "Even they stalled when they crossed over," I said.

Again that smile I loved so much. "And while we are flawed," he said with a shrug as if it didn't matter, so elegant and delicious in his expensive suit and tie, "our time has come at last."

"Creator did what She could with what She had," Alison said, smiling, taking Sebastian's hand. "She couldn't recreate the Order Herself, not when Her power was scattered, spread around the Universe. Instead, She gave that compulsion to Iepa of the maji."

Who made me. My vampire's voice was hard to hear she spoke so quietly.

And you, Moa spoke directly to her, *fulfilled the destiny She wanted of you exactly as it was meant to unfold.*

"But, that made us weaker than them." I gestured at the Order, the drachmor. Their power echoed from them, over us. Even in their frozen state they seemed larger than life, dominant, brutally strong.

"Not so," Sunny said, her brilliance outshining her name. "Because we were allowed to evolve, it is we who control this place." She gestured around her. "For now."

"We were the first to go," Sebastian said, "because we are them. Only better. Brighter." He laughed suddenly, shook his head. "All because you saved my life and gave mine back to me, Doombringer." Irony in those words, that title.

"I'm your doom," I said.

"All of ours," Alison said. "I couldn't think of a better doom for our race, could you?"

The Order shifted as one, stomping their feet before falling still again. The cries of the drachmor cut off, the sudden noise as terrifying as the instant silence. Sebastian turned toward the army of Dark Brother, face calm, almost serene.

"This is our task," he said. "Yours lies elsewhere, Sydlynn Hayle."

I didn't move, couldn't as the Order came to life again, this time not falling still as they had before, the drachmor screeching their fury at the drach on our side. I held my breath though the vampires around me—the Order of our Universe—strode ahead, standing rank upon rank against the enemy. Found myself in an eye blink on the edge of their pending battle, alone there, outside their fight. And shook in reaction to the sight of Oliver, his mother and a handful of their people—the damaged and wingless drach among them—as they crossed the firing line and joined Sebastian.

Against their own race.

It no longer felt like the coven site but a massive battlefield. And yet, no fight broke out, no war waged. Not yet. They hovered, waited, staring at each other across an invisible divide. I thought of the dream, of flying on drach back to my death dressed in Order armor, carrying a sword of light. Was this the moment of my own doom?

"Go now," Sebastian said, voice clear though it seemed he stood far away at the head of his own people. "Finish what you started."

"I can't leave you to fight them alone." I just couldn't.

"There will be no battle." Oliver spoke then, helmet pulled free, handsome face turned toward me. "Not until we know the final choice." He seemed stunned by that revelation. Shrugged. "Told you I'd see you on the other side."

This place was so odd, but I didn't complain when I found him instantly at my side. I hugged him hard. Welcomed his lips when he kissed me. And leaned away. Let my arms drop, felt my courage wane, lost and alone when he left me again, though I stood observing thousands.

"I don't know what to do." And hated being weak.

A voice snorted in my head, one I knew. But when I turned to look for Max, he wasn't there. And when the voice spoke clearly for the first time, I realized it wasn't my dear Max at all.

But the one I wore around my wrist.

Weak. How ridiculous. His tone was far more crisp, more youthful, less ponderous but no less powerful. *You are Doombringer. Now, move your ass and save the Universe.*

I felt him push me, propel me out of the coven site and staggered as I reappeared in my back yard.

Zoe waited there, Trill. But they weren't alone and I gaped at the sight of Mia standing next to Liander Belaisle who both smirked and looked nervous that Fate had finally brought us together again.

"It's time," Trill said. "Doombringer, the choice must be made."

TWENTY-NINE

I shivered but nodded, looking back and forth between Mia and Zoe, refusing to even glance at Belaisle. What was his role in this? I didn't want to know, though I suspected. Hated him for being here at all, as if I needed more reason for that hate beyond the usual.

Leave it to me to find more layers against him.

He was me, wasn't he? Okay, so face it then, Hayle. It was me and Zoe and Mia and him. But that left Trill… and Gabriel. I gasped when I remembered my son, bit my lower lip so hard it bled. How did I forget? How could I? My darling boy, my sweets, the soul of Creator, limp and dead in my arms as the Universe expired—

"Syd." Trill sighed. "I'm sorry." When she stepped aside I was surprised and, then again, not so much to see him there, smiling up at me.

Gabriel.

I laughed, ending in a gasp of grief that made my knees week. Needed to hug him. Not the time or place, was it? I held myself rigid, rooted on the spot. It was enough, had to be. He was safe, here with us. And I would do everything in my power to protect him from now on. His part was done. And mine was only beginning.

I faced down the Fates with grim determination I felt to the soles of my feet and through the three personas I carried with me. This was the moment, the time for which I'd been created. Everything that came before prepared me for now. My choice. Funny, I'd thought that one other moment in time, on the Stronghold plane with Belaisle and Demetrius and Max. New cast of characters added on for good measure, but more of the same.

I had this. I'd never felt so sure. Me, the girls, this Fate. We were ready to die, to let go, to do whatever they needed of us to fix the Universe. Anything.

"Tell me what to do," I said.

It was Gabriel who came to me, who took my hand in his. I squeezed reflexively, unable to stop myself. While I'd told myself seeing him alive was enough, I still fought the need to jerk him to me and hug him tight. He just kept smiling, sweet and loving.

"Not here," he said. "Let's go."

I let him lead me as Sebastian had led me, prepared this time for the journey through nothing that lasted less than an instant, eyes widening at the sight of the entrance to the cave. A giant rock had once blocked its entrance, where the Firbolg magician Cesard had been trapped for a thousand years. Along with the soul of the vampire now in my body and the twisted spirit of a demon lord.

"Why here?" Did it matter? I realized then, regardless of what anyone said, to me, always questioning, it did. The entrance beckoned, gaping black welcoming despite its darkness. This place had protected my family when the Brotherhood attacked, had been the hiding place of Sebastian when I'd saved him the first time. So many memories tied to it, back and back to the night when the cheerleader Suzanne cut herself around a campfire at a high school party and woke the power sleeping inside.

All of those memories jumbled into a ball of whirling confusion as Gabriel spoke.

"This is the place, Mom," he said. "The exact place where it happened."

Where what hap—

"Mom," Gabriel said while the ribbon around my wrist twisted in response. "Max."

Max?

The magicks.

"This is the place where Max split sorcery," I said in a breath of air that was surely my last because I was going to die of understanding right then and there. That's why it mattered, why it contained all the powers he'd created in that single act of curiosity that split the Universes. Why my plane seemed the center of so many things.

It was, literally.

Gabriel laughed, soft and bright. "It is," he said. "The native tribe who discovered this cave used it as a prison for the greatest darknesses they encountered. But it has been here, waiting for this day, since the instant Max divided the magicks. That same instant that held the Universes apart." Wait, what? That feeling of time forming the barrier was real? "The cave's lack of elemental magic comes from its task. To feed the barrier. It is, quite literally, the exact instant in time everything parted." He sounded so grown up, so sure of himself. "This is the moment and the place and the time, Mom. Now." He gestured upward, my eyes lifting to the sky. To the sight of the giant drach, wings out spread, a flare of white light rainbowing around him.

Silent. Still.

Max. So that's where he went.

Awe shook me, but I followed my son anyway because I was Doombringer and I'd come this far, hadn't I? Stumbling, in shock and not knowing how to feel outside of loving the boy who led me deep into the cave beneath Wilding Springs—into the moment of creation's dividing—I wasn't surprised to find Her waiting there.

But not a statue, no longer. Creator bowed Her head to me, massive form looming, gigantic presence so huge I could barely draw air into my lungs. When She gestured the air sang with Her motion, the void itself bending to Her perfection. Made worse by Her companion who lurked in the shadows, flames for eyes and the slash of His mouth belching smoke. Dark Brother.

I couldn't think or speak or move for a long time, held in place by the enormity of them, of this instant. It was Gabriel who finally prodded me to move, and Zoe and Mia, coming up behind us. The Fates passed me by, parting to stand before their patrons, Belaisle sullen in his subservient spot next to Mia. He felt insubstantial to me, as though his part in this were over but he didn't know it yet. I used to fear Belaisle, then hate him. In that moment, staring down the truth of who I was, I lost all animosity and even caring. All that was left was pity.

I was going to win. And, in winning, Belaisle would be nothing.

Nor was I terrified of Dark Brother any longer I realized as my son stood unwavering at my side, pulling me to a gentle halt before those who awaited us. Her sibling had no sway over me, His Fate more a threat—if Mia could be called that—than He would ever be.

And, for the first time, I felt the utter power that was being Doombringer. When I'd been called out to become the Light One, had been asked to give up everything to ensure the fulfillment of the prophecy, I'd done so willingly and ended up powerless for a time. This was utterly, completely different. My frightened mind stilled, retreated, the absolute rightness of who I was, of my task, taking over everything.

Only Trill seemed out of place, off to one side, her sad face forlorn but determined.

Gabriel squeezed my hand. I looked down at my son, smiled. Confidence took me, warmed me up, gave me voice.

"I love you, sweets," I said. I hadn't had a chance to answer him when he'd become Creator's last piece. It seemed immensely important I do so now.

"I know, Mom," he said, bright and shining, his father in the distance but all Gabriel. "I love you, too." Again he squeezed. "It's time to choose. For the two Universes to be made one again. Even if that means the end of one so the other can continue."

That was clear enough and, no offense to anyone present, but a no brainer as far as I was concerned. Still, I nodded, looked up at Creator who gazed at me with infinite caring and terrifying love. At Dark Brother and His flame filled face. And cleared my throat.

"I choose Creator," I said. And exhaled.

I'm not sure what I expected, but utter silence and nothing wasn't it.

Gabriel sighed, stepping away from me. Did he suddenly look older? Taller? Yes, he was growing, evolving before my eyes, his face Liam's face as he topped my height a moment later, looking about twenty-two or so, the age his father was when he died. I wept at the sight, hands shaking while I covered my mouth with both hands in an attempt to hold the sorrow in.

"I don't understand," I whispered. "I made my choice."

He shook his head, his father's eyes, Liam's voice and body, but my son shining through. "Mom," he said, deep and vibrating with emotion that pried my heart free from the terror that kept it trapped in my chest. "That's not your choice to make." What? He reached out to me, stroked hair from my cheek, smiled again. "That choice," he said. "It's mine."

His. Why his? Wait, then what did I have to...

"Sydlynn Hayle," Zoe said, Mia echoing her when Fate spoke from their lips. "Doombringer. Your choice is upon you. The destiny of the Universes lie in your hands. In your heart."

For the second time my soul screamed, *NO!* Even as my son bowed his head to me.

"In order to make my choice," he said. "I have to be free to do so. Doombringer, yours dictates if I can make mine."

Gabriel, Creator, Trill. Please. Anything but this.

"Mom," he whispered. "I can't be with you anymore. I have to stand alone." He shivered but didn't seem afraid, just sad, so sad. "You have to let me go."

THIRTY

I was going to throw up, fall down, die on the spot. Instead, my mouth opened and, in a calm voice that surely didn't belong to me, I asked the obvious. "Go? Go where?"

Sydlynn. Creator's voice was unmistakable as was the presence of Her mind in mine. Dark Brother's personality loomed behind Her, the scent of smoke strong in my senses as She went on. *No longer can we remain, my damned brother and I.*

Not both of us, He roared, though his tone was as low as Hers. It just came out that way, like a wildfire raging through a dying forest, chasing me down. But I had nowhere to hide.

Indeed. She nodded to Him while He seethed in fire. *If we attempt to combine as we are, we will destroy everything, the very reason I split Creation. Once separate, we could no longer become one again.*

Agreed, Dark Brother rumbled like an earthquake destroying a city of screaming people.

A new Creator must arise, She sent. *To take our place.*

Or not, Dark Brother hissed, pyroclastic cloud of death and destruction pouring from the top of a volcano.

We have agreed, the Fates sent, silencing them both. *Whatever the decision, when the choice is made, you will be gone and He will remain.* They were staring at my son.

My son.

The new Creator?

"I must choose which Universe shall remain," Gabriel said, backing away from me. Distancing himself in body and in soul. I could feel him pulling free, cutting ties to me. But I clung to him, couldn't release him. Not yet.

Maybe not ever.

Doombringer. Dear elements, now I understood. And it was the utmost of cruel evil they asked of me.

"When I choose," he said as if I didn't battle with him to hold him tightly to me, "one Universe will fall and the other will remain. And history will rewrite to encompass the new truth. No one but you and me—and a few others—will remember what used to be."

I shook my head, denial and pain and rejection all in that simplest of gestures. "No."

"You see?" Belaisle's voice held an oily cast I knew well, a conniving and convincing tone that made my skin crawl. How dare he speak to my son like that? "She will never let you go. You must let me kill her. Or all is lost."

Gabriel shook his head while Dark Brother chuffed agreement and Creator held still, silent, loving.

"She must choose," he said.

"I will not leave Fate in her hands," Belaisle growled, power seeping out.

Gabriel's magic clamped down on the old Brotherhood leader, Dark Brother's pawn collapsing to his knees with a scream of agony. But it was the Fates who spoke.

"Sydlynn Hayle," they said together, eyes glowing with the white sorcery I now knew was Creator's gift to all of us. Even the other Universe. "Choose. Release the Gateway to become Creator or be the Doombringer of all."

"Wait." Belaisle gasped for air, one last try to convince my son to let him kill me. But it was Dark Brother who acted this time, crushing Liander like a bug.

Silence, slave, He rumbled, a tsunami wiping out a civilization with a pounding wall of mile high water. *It is you who have failed in your task, thwarted by the deceit of the second race. The maji. Bellanca. Your life is mine, should the Gateway choose me.*

Belaisle shivered, blood seeping from his open mouth, one ear, the corner of his right eye. I almost felt sorry for him.

Liar.

Comfort is knowing your nemesis is a failure in the end. Though, torture is also knowing you might be, too.

"You understand now," Zoe said, herself for a moment, sad and hurt, "why we couldn't tell you anything?" She paused. "You who have given so much."

I did. If I'd known, I never would have started on this journey, would have told them all to hell with their choices and their Universes. It was too much, this loss. This thing they asked of me. After I'd given up Liam to Fate. They couldn't take my son, too.

"Gabriel." I choked on his name before my face crumpled in grief. "Tell me there's another way."

"I'm so sorry, Mom," he said, his beautiful eyes shining with tears. "There isn't. If you let me go, I become the Gateway to a new beginning and, upon choosing, I'm the new Creator."

I swallowed, nodded, amazed at my own calm. "And if I don't?"

You find out what being Doombringer really means, Creator sent.

It hit me then, like a punch to the gut, a slap to my face, a deathblow to my heart. What they really wanted me to do. Not some imagined possibility, or a chance of something happening. Reality took me by the spirit and shook me as hard as it could before dropping me back into this unbelievable situation to make a choice no mother should be asked to make.

You left me once before. It wasn't an accusation. Gabriel wasn't trying to hurt me. Just being reasonable, damn him. *Let me go, cut ties on purpose. When you joined the drach.*

With those who loved you. It came out in a wail. *Who could protect and adore you for me. This is different and you know it. This is...*

Final, he sent.

Oh, so final.

"No." I turned away, arms crossing over my chest less as a show of rebellion and more to keep myself from flying physically apart as I just held onto my ability to keep from screaming. "No, never, over my dead freaking body." I spun back into their silence, volume rising as I let out all my frustration and anger and the pent up piles of fury that had plagued me from the beginning while the girls within cowered in their grief at the thought of what was to come. "I will NEVER let him go. And after all that you've done, all that you've taken," I shook so hard my teeth rattled while I shrieked out the last of my protest, "HOW CAN YOU ASK THIS OF ME?"

Liam's face flashed in my head, Quaid, Ethie. Mom and Gram and Sass and Max and every single person I loved. Poor, dead Mia. The loss of the coven. All of it. One big ball of HELL TO THE *NO WAY*.

Then you are Doombringer no longer in name, Creator sent, not sad or judgmental, just stating facts. *But for real and for as long as we last here in this place.*

I swallowed convulsively, skin quivering, body shaking so hard I had to plant my feet wide apart to keep from falling. Not the ground moving. Just me, breaking down at last. At long last.

"Mom," Gabriel said. How dare he speak, try to convince me? He was my son, my sweets. Why did he want to leave me? "We can't stay here in the void much longer." No desperate plea, not from him. More truth, as calm as Her. I'd been seeing Her in him, thought it was the Universe, told myself it was the veil. Lied to myself over and over when it was clear, so clear now, who he was becoming.

What will happen? My vampire spoke up when I couldn't, didn't care or want to know. Didn't matter. Throw that back at Mia, at Trill and Zoe and Her. I'd never let him go.

"We will all fade away," Trill said. At least she had the decency to sound sad. "Lost to the darkness. And this Universe and its people will be gone forever."

So what? I turned my head, jaw set. So bloody what. "I'd rather that," I snarled, "than give up one more thing I love to you all." I slammed power into them, into the immovable wall of magic that stood before me while the ribbon on my wrist twisted its agony and the girls wept inside me. "I'd rather DIE than give you *ONE MORE THING.*" Didn't they see? Didn't they get it? The straw.

The camel.

Snap.

But they did see, didn't they? This was the cruel part, the damned rub of the whole business. The woman they'd made me with their manipulations and giant puppet strings and all the damned pathetic Fate crap that twisted me into a knot over and over again only to leave me out to dry. To figure things out for myself.

Pounding me into a shape they thought would give them what they wanted in the end.

"Screw you," I said.

Gabriel sighed, hung his head. "I'm the soul of Creation," he said, looking up again to meet my eyes. "A gift from my father and you, born of your combined power and the veil thanks to his sacrifice and the Gates of the Sidhe." No, he did not try to convince me. "This is my destiny, Mom. And like it or not, we Hayles have to follow the path we've been set upon. Don't we?" He shrugged as if he didn't like it but had no choice. I knew that feeling intimately. "We're nothing if not predictable when it comes to Fate."

We always do the right thing. Well, too bad. Not this time.

Never again.

I love you, he whispered in my mind and I broke down completely, Shaylee wailing in the back of my mind, my demon sobbing as though she'd never be free of her hurt, my vampire turning away to hide behind my dying heart. *You raised me to do this, Mom. To say yes. And I know whatever choice you make, it's the right one.* He paused before going on in a rush. *I know as much as you love me, too, you're also a Child of Creator. And we stick together, don't we?*

Sob.

I'll always be with you. His heart hugged mine before he stopped. Waited. And smiled at me with Liam's face.

Oh, my love. What do I do?

I felt it then, the clash of the armies, the hit of power as the war began. Drach against drachmor, vampires against the Order. More suffering, more death, even here, in the void. Did they know what they fought for didn't have value? Sebastian said the war wouldn't happen until the choice was made. I guess I'd made mine, then. Or had I? Saying no didn't seem to be the final answer, regardless their fight waging out there, in the dullness of nothing.

So, here I was. With a simple choice I could end their strife. Or do nothing and let it continue until they faded away into the darkness.

My weeping stopped of its own accord, my heart slowing its pounding. Choice waited as I hovered, eyes on the floor, decision made. Not made. Made. Not made. And the war went on and on, two fronts a battlefield I'd not recover from.

The Universe slipped. Just a little a fraction, a faded edge gone into the dark forever. I knew it was forever, that I'd just doomed a small plane and its inhabitants to nothingness. No history, no one to remember they existed. And that awaited everyone I loved, everyone I knew.

Selfish and furious and full of the need to hurt someone, I slashed at the connection to my son and severed our link in an impulsive burst of hate. No choice. Never a choice. Better bitterness and blame than this hole in my heart that would never heal.

"Go," I snarled at him, at them. "Take him as you always planned. Do your worst. I'm done."

THIRTY-ONE

It didn't matter how I felt about it, how the fury ran out of me the moment I cut ties with my son for the second time, for the last time. How my heart went with that cruelest of gestures, crumbled to dust in my chest. When I'd left him to join the drach it had been for his good, at least from what I'd told myself at the time. To protect him, his sister. Myself from the hurt I'd accrued. And I guess I never truly believed I'd never see him again. He'd been there, at home, waiting for the day maybe I could figure out a way to go back. And that was just what happened.

This time? This felt like forever. Was forever. Just the fact I had no choice made it all the harder to swallow. Stubborn, caustic, bullheaded Sydlynn Hayle. Creator made me this way. I would blame Her for as long as I lived.

However long that ended up being.

Gabriel turned from me, expanding upward until he dwarfed Creator and Dark Brother with his size. Or, did they shrink, too? Possibly. Probably. All I know is, moments later, I gaped up at him as he cupped Her in one hand and Him in the other, a glowing light balanced by a dark flame dancing over his knuckles. Liam's giant face smiled kindly down on those who had been the driving force of creation since there was a creation as if he were their kindly grandfather.

Shudder.

"Tell me," he said in his father's voice. "Why I should choose you?"

Creator's sibling wasted no time getting His word in edgewise. *My Universe is the true Universe*, Dark Brother sent, fire and brimstone of hell bubbling under the surface. *Sorcery the one real power united, never divided, clean and pure. My Order are the soldiers intended to protect all creation, the drachmor their companions.*

"Stolen from my Universe. You liar." I seethed while Gabriel's gigantic gaze turned to me, his immense power washing over me. I would never, ever, bring myself to use the capitalized pronoun for him, no matter what happened. He was my son. Creator or not, Gabriel would remain my sweets to me forever.

"Your part is done, Sydlynn Hayle," he said like I'd

never been his mother. Huff.

Chastised, I turned away, not caring anymore. Telling myself that just to get through the next breath, the next heartbeat. To find Trill had come to my side. I wasn't sure I wanted her there, but couldn't bring myself to turn away. She ignored Dark Brother as He went on like nothing He said mattered, His litany of awesomeness going on and on so long I was sure if I had to listen to Him say one more word about how amazeballs His Universe was I'd start screaming again.

"You can blame me," she said like we were alone over a cup of coffee and she'd only come for a casual visit. "If it makes you feel better."

I wished it would, could find some way to turn her offer into a truth that could rouse me to anything but hurt. "I left him once before," I said, dead and dull, accepting. And hating that attitude so much I finally found a spark of anger again. Only to lose it as I glanced up and absorbed the giganticness that was my son. "So I guess it shouldn't have been so hard to do."

Shouldn't have been. But was.

Trill hesitated before hugging me while Dark Brother finally wound up His droning, commanding speech about His perfect awesomesauceness. "It'll be okay," she whispered like she believed it.

She was wrong, though. Things would never be okay. Ever again. But I nodded instead of telling her that truth, in the end giving her the comfort she needed though she hadn't earned it from me. I was too tired and wrung out, too in shock and long past broken to find words to fight back against the lie she tried to hide in a hug and her dark eyes. And turned back with her when Dark Brother fell silent.

"I have heard you," Gabriel said, his voice a waterfall and a whispered breeze carrying the scent of lilacs. That brought tears to my eyes. Made me think of Mom, her strength, how she always held it together no matter what. I'd learned from the best, could wear that mask of control if I chose to. Okay, I could do this. For Mom and Dad and Meems. I could. If it meant they'd be okay in the end, even if I wasn't. And my daughter. For Ethie.

Who would never forgive me for losing her brother like this.

"Creator," my son—no, not my son anymore. The Gateway nodded to Her. "Speak. Why should I choose you?"

You shouldn't, She sent.

Gasp. *What the hell is wrong with Her?* I spun on Trill who shook her head, tired and sad.

Just listen, she sent.

"Explain," the Gateway said as Dark Brother chortled, bubbling caldera of magma heating His joy.

My time is done, She sent. *So, choose not me. Choose those whose evolution has created some of the most amazing and spectacular events in my Universe's history. The good and the bad.*

Choke. Okay, She got me as She flashed images at him, at all of us. Of the moment Max split the powers, the creation of Demonicon and its Node holding all those planes together. The Stronghold, the drach and, yes, even the maji. The evolution of the drachmor before they left us, witches and sorcerers and vampires and werewolves. Variety, diversity, magic beyond the power of sorcery. I wept again, caught tears trickling from my eyes as Her final image landed on Liam. *Sacrifice and kindness*, She sent, *and the souls of those who would give anything for each other.* To Max and then Sassafras. To Charlotte, my mother. And, finally, to me.

She fell silent while Gabriel pondered and Dark Brother huffed.

Ridiculous, He snarled, a savage hoard overtaking a desperate village.

Perhaps, She sent. *But beautiful all the same.*

He held silent, the soul that had been my son and was Creator all along. And, as I watched him, as he struggled with his choice, I felt my anger retreat, my loss ebb, the core of my hate die. While empathy soared alongside the pride I still felt, despite myself, for the boy who had been Gabriel Liam Hayle. He was amazing and immense, vast and stunning in his power, and still, always I hoped, to his core the dear, dear heart I knew and loved.

Could I live with what I'd done? I didn't know. But,

in that moment as the Gateway decided, I knew I'd made the right decision after all. No matter the consequences to me personally.

Look at me, being all self-sacrificing and accepting and stuff.

Trill twitched beside me and I spared her a glance. Tears trickled down her cheeks, her face full of regret. But it was the touch of his mind that made me gasp, that pulled me around and forced me to focus.

I thought I was going to choose Her, Gabriel sent directly to me. From his touch this was a private conversation, so massive I almost couldn't comprehend the fact he had turned to me, his mom, in the end. *I had a plan. But now I'm not so sure.*

Yes, you are, my vampire sent.

You've always been sure, my demon told him.

You are the Gateway. Shaylee's power stroked him with kindness and love. Her own pride. *As much as your mother, you were made for this. And the truth of what you must do lives in you as surely as it lives in her.*

At least someone has faith in me, he sent and I choked on a laugh.

Sounds familiar, I sent. *I say that to myself all the time.* Paused and tried to gather myself. *This is your choice,* I sent.

Yes, he sent. *But you're my mother, like it or not.*

You know what I would do, I sent. *Who I'd choose.*

I do. He chuckled. *You already told us, remember?*

Are you going to listen to your mother? Where had this humor come from past the hurt and the loss? One last moment with the beautiful boy I loved.

He hesitated. And then joy blossomed in him. *I am,* he sent. *But not the way you expect. Because you are unexpected. And I love you for it.*

I had no idea what that meant and hoped I hadn't led him astray. Or that my influence was about to lead us into disaster.

What, foster disaster? Me? What else was new?

I've chosen. His vast mind swelled inside the cave, embraced all of us, even the crippled and bleeding Belaisle. The void seemed to hold still in that instant, breath drawn, waiting. The battle outside stilled, Order and drachmor, vampires and drach stopped, listening. I found myself doing the same, chest tight past the aching of my lungs as I anticipated what growing up Sydlynn Hayle's daughter might mean for the new Creator's decision.

Oh boy. We were in so much trouble.

I felt a giggle of hysterical denial burble in my stomach as Creator bowed Her head to Gabriel, Dark Brother grumbling, fire seeping free.

When you're left without a choice, my son said—because make no mistake, it was my son that said it, *hell* yeah—*you make your own way.* He laughed, power engulfing them. *I choose you both.*

THIRTY-TWO

Fate's response was immediate and horrified. "No!" They shouted that word together even as the powers that were Creator and Dark Brother flared with magic. "You must choose!" I felt Dark Brother's rejection of my son's choice, His attempt, even in this juncture, to deceive and betray. How His energy writhed with fury and fought against the ruling as though He had planned to win all along. Of course He had. But Gabriel, my Gabriel, was far too strong.

As for Her, the touch of Creator's joy was enough to bring more tears to my eyes.

I chose well, She sent to me as Her magic flared and vibrated, Her form spinning toward Her dark sibling while He snarled and fought against the inevitable. No matter His plans, his vast conniving, not even He could defeat Fate and the Gateway.

Belaisle screamed his agony as Dark Brother took His power back in a jerk of resentful spite, the small form of my old enemy collapsing at last on the cold rock, motionless.

I could do nothing but stand there, hugging myself, feeling the pressure of what was coming build inside me, outside me, grateful to be there in the end, to know my death meant the Universe would survive. Because surely I wouldn't. Something hot ran down my upper lip and I tasted blood in the back of my throat, my chest caving in while I sagged to my knees. The Fates were screaming, clutching at their temples while their eyes ran crimson rivers and the massive, towering presence that was Gabriel took on all that was and would ever be. In both Universes.

Impossible, surely this was the death of everything. The end. Because both could not exist in one place. Creator had said it. Insisted on it. The very reason She split the Universes was to protect them from this possibility. Combination would mean destruction.

Wouldn't it? If so, why then did She seem so pleased with my son's choice?

When white light flared, the perfect source of all Creator's magic engulfing me, I realized the dream I'd had was altered. The end was still coming. But I had no armor to shield me in the last moment, no drach mount to share my death. Only my son, his eyes full of the stars smiling down at me in the final instant.

I died to the sound of Trill laughing.

When I opened my eyes, the sky overhead had regained its brilliant blue. The cool air rushed over me, the grass under my head and hands crisp and dead from an early frost. Not summer, not the strange, dull place I'd been before. I blinked into the bright sunlight of late October, chest heaving a breath, another. It took everything I had just to sit up, my strength easing slowly back into my shaking limbs, while a pair of blue jays chattered at a cawing crow over a scrap of something in the corner of the yard.

The air in my lungs tasted fresh, light. When I could raise my hands, they ran over my face, finding clean skin, no blood. Stunned, trembling, I sat there a long time, pulling my knees to my chest as I tried to tie together the pieces of what just happened.

The Universe. It was whole again. I felt the veil, the steadiness of it, its content and joy, as always. As if nothing—and everything—had changed. I reached for the rubbery membrane and, in doing so, felt the drachmor in a flare of fear that faded when their presence vanished from my touch. Gone, but where? There, the Order, their towering power no longer a threat. The vampires, equals. Vampires no longer, I guess. That would take getting used to. What else had changed?

My heart flinched as I dodged the obvious, the girls silent within me, turning away from what none of us could face just yet. Instead, we chose together to dig deeper into the alterations to my normal instead of facing what I'd lost by choice. Made it a little better the souls of those I loved, all the ties and links and connections, were there again, stronger than ever, fed through the pulse of the power of white sorcery. It permeated every single cell of every single plant, animal, person. As if it had always been.

I understood then what my son had accomplished as the Universe spun outward, vast initially, even more so now.

A miracle. Fate's fears unfounded, obviously. Gabriel's choice was the right one after all. So, what had them terrified in his moment of choice? What kept them from rejoicing at his decision to make both Universes whole?

I'd find out. Soon. Once I was able to stand up and function and even accept what had happened.

The back door opened, instinct turning my head at the sound. A sob caught in the back of my throat at the sight of Mom standing there, her eyes wide, her mouth an "O" of surprise.

"Syd!" She hurried toward me, her velvet skirt whispering in the still air, her approach chasing off the battling birds. I wondered in absent confusion who won, the jays or the crow while my mother sank to the ground and embraced me, pressing my cheek to her shoulder as she crouched at my side. The scent of lilacs took me back, way back, to childhood and summer and endless love. "Sweetheart." She leaned away, touching my cheeks with warm fingers, concern on her face. "What happened?" She examined my torn t-shirt, my filthy jeans, hair full of rock dust from the destruction of the Stronghold's underchamber. That happened, didn't it?

Didn't it?

From the way she looked at me, she had no idea what I'd just been through. We had a lot to talk about, clearly. That conversation felt entirely reasonable until she opened her mouth and asked her final question. "Are you all right?"

I shook my head, memory zinging painfully, not sure what to tell her, not even certain I could speak past my instantly tight throat and aching chest. I managed a nod, mind whirling, everything going black around the edges a moment while I drew in a final cleansing breath and accepted what just happened.

Because it did happen. I had no doubt whatsoever. She was alive, they all were. No burning sky above a bubble of protective power. No crumbling veil falling into the void. My world, the Universe, intact. Gone the burned out shell of war, the devouring draw of nothingness. Here, real. Whole and well. All because of him.

And Doombringer.

I wept then, for my loss, for Fate and the choices I'd been forced to make. Having no choice at all. I fell onto my mother's shoulder with grief eating me alive while the Universe sighed and spun and lived around me.

THIRTY-THREE

I stood outside his cell, nothing about this feeling right or normal, as the Enforcer guard unlocked it and let me inside. His young face seemed nervous, as if I was a loose cannon and a threat. Maybe he was right to be afraid. I'd just single handedly decided the fate of the Universes, hadn't I? That thought stirred hysterical giggles, barely contained. Did I look manic, insane to him? Possibly.

Probably.

I knew this prison, had been here before but under circumstances that had allowed the former wereking, Danilo Moreau, to escape with his sister. In search of answers we still didn't have.

They didn't matter now, my new favorite saying. Not when I passed the frightened young guard, Mom waiting for me outside the door, into the bright, white interior of the ten by ten space. He sat at the table with his big, tanned hands folded in front of him, the cream cotton of his jumpsuit baggy on his large form. I sank into the wobbly metal chair across from him, hesitant and afraid.

"Syd." Quaid's voice cracked. He cleared his throat and tried again, a faint smile on his lips, chocolate eyes heavy lidded as he reached out and took my hand. So warm his skin on my icy fingers. Like we still had feelings for each other. "You shouldn't be here."

I shrugged, looked away, unable to meet his gaze any longer. I had to tell him what happened. How could I? Admit to him that his son—by love if not by blood—was gone forever, the new Creator of our Universe? He'd hate me, go to his execution knowing I'd failed our family for the last time. How could I make him carry that burden? But he deserved to know.

"I had to see you." That sounded weak in my own ears, small and frail compared to the weight of what I was about to drop between us. I forced my head around, met his gaze as my demon whispered her comfort, Shaylee hugging me with earth magic, my vampire silent, watchful. Quaid might not be mine anymore but he was my husband once, loved my son like his own. And he deserved to hear the truth from me. "To tell you what happened."

Quaid frowned. "I know what happened," he said, gruff and cold. "I was there. Tallah killed Varity. And I murdered her on purpose, intentionally, in revenge." He shrugged his broad shoulders, his turn to look away. "And I'll burn for it. There's nothing you can do to stop it."

It took me a moment to shift from my own burden to his. So he didn't know anything had changed. I shivered, removed my hands from his. He didn't try to reach for me again, sitting back with his arms crossed over his chest, dark hair shaggy over his brow.

"Gabriel is gone," I whispered. Choked on it. I hadn't talked to Mom about it, couldn't bring myself to talk to anyone. This was the first time since I opened my eyes in the back yard—was it only two hours ago?—I admitted my son's loss. "And it's my fault."

Quaid frowned, deep and penetrating, turning back to stare at me. "What?"

I nodded, swallowed hard. "I had to choose," I said, hearing the tears in my voice, not sure I could finish speaking, sure those tears would silence me into a bout of sobbing so powerful I'd never, ever stop. But I managed, with their help, the girls supporting me with their love and acceptance, enough I could get out the last words before grief shut me down. "Doombringer chose. And doing so meant setting him free to be Creator."

Quaid's frown turned to concern as he leaned toward me, hands dropping to the table with two loud thuds. "Syd," he said. "What are you talking about?"

I froze into quiet, grief gone suddenly, entire body still. And understood what I hadn't yet grasped. Took on, in that moment of frozen time, the utter and absolute agony that was the truth of what I'd done. Beyond anything I'd first conceived, past the initial pain of losing my son. I'd done more than that, much worse than I'd ever imagined possible.

He'd warned me himself. Told me, hadn't he? Gabriel said it, but I hadn't heard him, not really. My son. The search for the pieces. The fall of the Universe. Erased with his choice. And mine. Along with him.

I couldn't breathe, didn't want to live anymore. How could I have made the choice I did? How could I not know doing so would mean rewriting everything? That letting my son go meant he never existed?

Quaid leaned away again, hands falling into his lap. He stared down at them, frown still in place. "Whatever," he said. "It doesn't matter now." There was that phrase again. "None of it does. Except one thing." His eyes flickered upward, meeting mine with a burning passion so powerful I couldn't deny him, not after what I'd done. "I'll be dead in three days," he said, level and confident in his own demise. I didn't argue, just held still and shook and tried to listen while my mind whispered to me over and over how wretchedly horrible I truly was. Doombringer. "I don't matter now. I'll pay for what I did, gladly. Varity." He choked, stopped. Shook his head and forged on. "My fault." He knew the blame game as intimately as I did. "And I'd do it again. Take Tallah out. But Syd. I need to know she's safe."

Varity? She was dead. And then it hit me. "Payten," I whispered. The babies.

He nodded, face crumpling an instant, so fast it was gone again before I could react to his deep and terrible grief. It felt like mine. "Protect her," he said. "Them. You have no reason to care about her. Or my kids." I nodded, wiped at the stray tear that escaped, swallowed the giant lump and took on his pain willingly. Just in case doing so might help me shake off my own. "In fact, I know you have reason to hate her." He paused again, lower lip trembling as he ran one hand over his cheek, fingers rough on the stubble there. The rasping sound was loud in the room, our combined breathing sounding like a wild animal panting in panic. "She'll want to see me," he said. "Don't let her. Just let me go."

"She's a Hayle, now," I said. "So are the kids." It seemed important he know that.

Quaid sobbed once, caught himself, looked away as he clutched at his own body with his hands and arms, hugging himself like he hugged them instead. "Thank you," he whispered, hoarse and full of regret. "Now get the hell out of here. I never want to see you again."

I staggered to my feet, the legs of the chair scraping over the white floor with a horrible sound.

"And if you show up at my execution," he said, voice dropping low, command there as he stared with that intensity I remembered so well, "I'll set the fire myself. Don't try to see me. Don't try to save me. Just get out. And keep them safe."

I fell into Mom as I left the room, barely remembering exiting the space, the clang of the door heavy behind me. She held me against her, leading me down the corridor, her shaking matching mine so we staggered as we went.

I just spoke to Femke, she sent, even her mental voice shivering with shock. *She refuses to commute his sentence.*

He murdered a witch in vengeance in front of dozens of witnesses, Mom, I sent, feeling dullness replace the grief inside me. I grasped for it, pulled it to me like a cloak. I'd take it over the hurt. Calm settled and I inhaled before going on. *Even if Femke was herself she'd be hard pressed to find an excuse not to execute him.*

Mom shuddered while I led her into the veil and opened the way back to Harvard. At least the WPC leader hadn't tried to arrest me or attack me when I was there. Even let me see Quaid. Oh, wait. History was rewritten. Did that mean I wasn't thinking straight? Was Femke okay after all?

But Mom nodded her agreement as she sank into her office chair. "We need to deal with Femke's situation," she said, confirming my friend was still under the control of Konstantin's soul. "I'm just…"

Tired. So tired. I turned to the window, stood next to the tall glass and looked out into the world that spun on without me for the moment. "I know. One thing at a time." I liked this dull feeling, sank deeper into it. Relief, like a gray blanket of kindness, kissed my cheek and let me think. "Mom." I had to know. But asking would mean stirring the hurt again. Still. "Do you remember Gabriel?"

She looked up as I glanced over at her, chest tightening against her response. She frowned, shook her head. "Who, sweetheart?"

There it was, the agony, rising up to take my soul. I jerked at the gray blanket and fell into its folds. That was better. Stillness calmed all of us, the girls as eager as I was to rest in its embrace.

"Never mind," I said.

"I'm not prepared to quit," Mom said, determination firing in her power, in the magic of the council. "There are old laws I can still dig through, exceptions can be made. I can hold off his execution for a little while, at least." She wrung her hands in her lap, giving in to tears for a moment before her confidence returned. A mask I knew well, had used myself a time or two. Learned from her. "If you can find a way to heal Femke, maybe Quaid can be saved."

Right. There was more to do. That understanding hit me harder than the grief. I looked out into the fall sunshine and tried to care.

Failed.

Blamed Fate and Creator. Why the hell couldn't the whole Universe rewrite have just fixed Femke already? Hadn't I earned that much? Bitterness colored the gray place and sparked a memory. I'd welcomed it in before, hadn't I? Been here. When I thought Gabriel died, a stolen infant replaced by the body of a normal child seeded to feel like my son. How fitting it was that same dullness and lack of giving a crap that would save me now.

The door to Mom's office vibrated with a magical knock. Her soft *come* preceded the portal opening, a tall, attractive young woman stepping through. She wore the black robe of an Enforcer, the blue bands at her wrists marking her as the new leader. I didn't know her, didn't bother introducing myself as she glanced at me with shock before bowing her head to Mom.

"Forgive me, Council Leader," she said in a voice that would have sounded more normal coming from a man. Deep, resonant, powerful.

"It's all right, Beverley," Mom said. "What is it?"

"The council has assembled," the young Enforcer leader said, crisp and professional. "They await you in the chamber."

Mom sighed, nodded. "I'll be right there." Beverley left, closing the door firmly behind her. "Beverley

Villard." I didn't know that family name. "She came highly recommended from Varity." Mom's voice cracked. "So hopefully she'll work out."

"That's nice." It was all I could muster. "I have to go." Before she discovered I didn't care. Would likely never care again, about anything. I should have been curious about what the combination of the Universes meant, what changes to history might have come about. But I just couldn't bring myself to stir any interest.

Mom didn't speak as I parted the veil and left her there.

THIRTY-FOUR

The moment I stepped into the veil, I felt her. Shuddered from the contact but she didn't seem interested in what I wanted. Trill appeared at my side, one hand grasping my elbow. I didn't bother trying to pull away, layering more dullness over my consciousness. Maybe if I wasn't available she'd just leave me alone.

Maybe they all would.

But I could tell from the grim determination on her face Trill Zornov wasn't going to let me get away with checking out just yet.

Anger flared then, and I welcomed its old familiar friendship. *How could they not remember him?* I threw that demand at her, hit her with it like a blow.

Trill seemed to expect the attack, took it and absorbed it. *That's how it had to be, Syd.*

Not good enough. I snarled in her face, wanting to hit her for real, needing to strike out and hurt someone, anyone, take down a mountain, destroy a plane, tear the Universe itself apart again.

No. Calm. Dull. Gray. There, yes. Better.

Trill seemed shocked by my sudden retreat, concern on her face, but she spoke anyway, firm and powerful. *He is Creator,* she sent. *And while they might not remember him or anything that happened, he is here, now. With us. And always will be.*

Oh, shut up. I turned from her, pulling free at last. *You're so full of crap. Just leave me alone, Trill. I'm done.*

It doesn't work that way. How dare she use that tone with me? I spun back to her, my demon snarling, Shaylee rumbling with anger. Only my vampire seemed quiet and calm.

It does, I sent through a clenched mind, *if I say it does.*

You don't get it. Trill's anger answered mine. *Stop being selfish and look around you.* Her hands flew out at her sides while I burned at her choice of words. Selfish? *SELFISH?* She went on as if she wasn't aware I was two shakes from going nuclear on her ass. *Everything is different, Syd. But everything is the same.*

Bullshit, I snapped. *No one remembers what happened. No one remembers him. It's like he never existed and his sacrifice is for nothing.* Be honest, Syd. With yourself, if no one else. Not his, that wasn't the hurtful part. *My* sacrifice.

It had to be this way. Trill wasn't about to soften the blow. Did she know trying to be kind wouldn't reach me? Likely. I hated her for knowing me so well, for manipulating me into caring even this little bit. Well, we'd see about that.

Okay then, I sent. *If you say so.*

She exhaled harshly, shook her head so her dark hair rippled around her. *What we did. What he did. Syd, we saved everything.*

That's nice. Now she was irritated. Awesome. *And who are you in all this again?* She flinched, looked away. *Right, sorry, never mind. You can't tell me. Because Fate and crap.* I barked a laugh into her head, hoped it hurt. *I'm done being a toy, Trill. So you can take your terrible attempt at bringing me back into the fold and shove it up your ass.*

They'll never know, she whispered it, like it hurt her, too. No way. No empathy. And yet, how much had she lost, given up, sacrificed? I had no idea. Because she wouldn't tell me. Way to waffle back and forth between being human and a bitch, Syd. *And it's better that way.* Her dark eyes were sad again. I grit my teeth against compassion. *So odd to feel them, don't you think?* She showed me faces I knew well. Sebastian and Mom and Mabel. They were themselves. But more. I could see that now. And gasped at the sight of two people, once belonging to separate Universes, their souls now inhabiting one body.

This can't be good.

Trill sighed. *It's why the Fates argued against his choice. But he had no alternative.*

He could have let the Dark Universe go. Logic, yup. And a bit of bias. So sue me.

Trill flinched, looked away. *Not yet,* she whispered.

Like hell this wasn't over. *Just tell me,* I sent. *Or get lost.*

She seemed to consider it but finally shrugged. *Gabriel did his best. And it's enough.*

For now, I sent.

She didn't answer. She didn't have to.

Well, whatever you have planned, I sent, spinning from her and reaching for the veil, *whoever you really are, Trill, that you think you have control over the Universe and Creator, you can leave me out of it from now on.*

I'll be seeing you, she said, wistful and full of sorrow.

Not if I can help it.

I stepped through the veil, leaving her behind.

THIRTY-FIVE

Home. I sat on the bench in the back yard, staring into the darkness as night descended, layering deeper and deeper filters of gray over me while the girls whispered their grief to each other. Better not to feel, not right now. Maybe later. I had eternity, didn't I? To process and work things out. Surely I deserved a little bit of relief no matter what I had to do to get it.

Betrayal I'd not been allowed my final battle, my ride into light and death with my drach mount beneath me, felt like the Universe itself had let me down. The dream, the precog glimpse of the future, felt like a slap to my face, to my commitment to Creator and Fate.

Well, screw it.

His fat cat body landed in my lap, purr starting the instant his feet touched down, but I blocked the power behind it, smothered the caring and kindness he tried to share. The rumble stopped after a few seconds as he gave up and sighed.

"Syd," Sass said. "What's going on?"

I shook my head. "It doesn't matter," I said. I'd have that tattooed on me somewhere, someday. "You don't remember." Damn, where did those tears come from? Lock them down, wrap them in dullness, still your heart.

"Remember what?" He wasn't about to give up and I just couldn't have that. "Syd, we're all worried about you. It's like you just suddenly broke." Sass's voice cracked. "For no reason."

No reason. I wanted to crush him for that, to grind him into a wet paste of fur and blood and bone, rage a fire that would not die no matter how much gray I embraced. Instead, I pushed him firmly and unceremoniously off my lap and heard him thud to the ground at my feet with a huff of surprise.

"Just leave me alone." Was I imagining the puff of mist that left my lips as I spoke? Might be that cold out. Or maybe it was my tone.

He stayed there a moment, indecision hanging between us. And then, with a mournful sigh, he slunk away, head low, tail between his legs.

I let him go. No remorse, no empathy, no compassion. No kindness. Nothing was allowed in.

I should have expected him to be next, but I still

caught my breath when the tall, handsome man who smelled of fabric softener and felt like a pillar of steel sat next to me and stared into the darkness without a word. Oliver. Of all people. Why did he raise an emotion in me when those I loved the most in the world couldn't?

History. What happened between us in his memory? Did he know anything or was he as ignorant of my loss as the others? Likely the latter. I couldn't bring myself to ask him.

"I can't give you what you want." Going to nip this in the bud right now, before he spoke, before he offered his heart. Because he was here for that, I had no doubt. Could feel him acutely, painfully, next to me. "So you might as well just go."

Oliver inhaled. Exhaled. "I know you'll never get over losing him," he said as my head whipped around. "And I wouldn't ask you to." His gray eyes met mine, level and quiet. "It's hard, being the only ones who know what happened. I figured you could use someone to talk to."

Choke. "You. Remember." Gabriel.

Oliver nodded as my son's words came to me again, torture, sweet torture. "There's a few of us Creator left aware," he said, shattering the protections I'd built as easily as if I'd made them of fluff and wishes. "So you wouldn't be alone, I guess."

No, please. Just let me have this retreat.

"I don't want to remember." I'd never forget. But my

best case scenario was being destroyed by his kindness. I didn't want that, either. Couldn't bear it.

"You will. One day." He held my hand, squeezed. And hate surged through our connection, hit his heart directly as I rejected him and everything he offered me.

Oliver flinched, paled. I watched with the need for cruelty while his face crumpled then stilled, observed with the desire to hurt as the love he was about to offer shriveled and retreated in exquisite agony.

"I'm sorry," he said. Staggered to his feet. Left me there, the door banging shut behind him. Even as a tiny corner of my soul wept at his going. At what I'd just done to him.

To hell with him. But now I knew there were others who shared my memories, I reached for the one I was sure would know all. As he'd always known. With the need to torment him, too.

Max's mind welcomed me, though from the way he felt he expected my fury.

YOU LED ME TO THIS, I sent with blow after blow following each word. *FROM DAY ONE. YOU LET THIS HAPPEN.* He finally flinched but didn't back down, taking every hit with his normal stoic nature. That just made my fury worse. *YOU KNEW.*

I did. No apology, no guilt. *Some, at least. Enough to know what would happen in the end.*

I hit him as hard as I could across the distance, not

even capable of gathering myself to fly through the veil and take it out on him physically. The ribbon on my wrist flexed in sympathy, begged me silently to stop. I abandoned my attack on Max, that immovable damned juggernaut of lies and deceit, and clawed at the drach soul that was his twin as it clung to my flesh.

It, at least, refused to go, and I finally quit, panting and filled with rage.

Syd. My demon's fury matched mine. *Stop.*

What? How could she demand that of me?

Syd. Shaylee's rumbling voice quieted as she hugged me tight. *Please.*

No, they couldn't turn on me, too. They had to feel the way I did.

Syd. My vampire. The source of the Order. She felt different, altered. The same, though. Part of me. *We love you. Don't let this break you.*

Too late. I sagged into the bench. *Too late.*

They wept with me, then, for our loss, for the end of what we'd known. While the damned Universe spun on as if nothing had happened.

THIRTY-SIX

The gray called and I answered.

Didn't matter Ethie hated me for not saving her father. My daughter's fury and tears did nothing to reach through the newly reinforced layers of safety from feeling I'd managed to create. She could scream at me and throw things all she wanted. Her father was going to die and there was nothing I was going to do about it.

Could have, maybe. If I cared. I didn't.

Not even that she'd bonded so deeply with Payten and the babies. Gorgeous girls, both of them. I think Quaid's wife named them but I couldn't remember what they were. Oh, well. Like it mattered. I was doing my part, keeping them safe like he asked. Quaid said nothing about actually giving a crap otherwise.

Nice of him.

I stopped looking for those who might remember

Gabriel and the search for Creator's pieces. Again, didn't matter. Asking meant staring and blank expressions followed by concern for my mental health. Whatever. Besides, it didn't really change anything, did it? I couldn't reverse it, take back my choice. And this depth of unfeeling was equal to the void, in my opinion. Maybe if I stayed here long enough I'd fade away, just like I'd been told the Universes would if I didn't give up my son.

Not going there.

Sassafras was gone, living in the Stronghold with Jiao. Abandoned the family, the traitor. Let him leave. Not like the coven needed him anymore. I sure didn't.

As for Oliver, he never came back. Probably for the best. I was sure his life was better without me in it.

So hard to care when they came to me with their troubles, filling me in like they always did with what was going on in their petty, small, pathetic lives. Piers and Demetrius and their Sorcerers League. Children playing at power. Mom and her struggles with the covens, the other territories. Seriously, they all needed to grow the hell up. Femke and the soul of Konstantin embedded in her. Sad, I guess. But not my problem.

Sebastian and Alison seemed to think I needed to be part of the Order, but I blocked that as soon as it was broached. No way. Autonomy from now on. They could have their precious collective. I'd told Trill I was done. I meant it.

Mabel's announcement Max stepped down as leader of the drach hit me harder than I should have let it. Took extra swaddling of dim uncaring to cut that cord of giving a crap. Whatever his reasons, he was probably right to do so. He'd been in power too long. Made a right mess of things. And without wings? Inferior.

Okay, that was cruel. Even I admitted that in the privacy of my heart. And wished things were different. That I could go to him and convince him otherwise. But I just couldn't allow even that to come between me and my newfound peace.

I couldn't even raise curiosity at the continued absence of the maji. The missing drachmor. And Ameline. As far as I was concerned, they'd burned themselves up at last and were long gone. Good freaking riddance to rubbish that should have been tossed ages ago.

There was a brief moment I considered talking to Queen Aoilainn about Liam. But the truth would shatter my retreat. He was gone, I had to face that. And doing so in the gray was way easier.

It was getting harder and harder to stay connected to the world around me. Good enough. I'd take it. Sink into my pillow and the comfort of my quilt, pull the covers over my head and exhale myself into the quiet air of my bedroom. They'd stopped coming to see me since I locked my door and warded it with magic.

So tired. I just needed to sleep for a little while. And dream, maybe.

No. Dreaming was bad. Painful. Reminded me that, in the end, I'd lost so much.

Better the gray and the stillness and silence. But he haunted me, wouldn't let me go, came to me when I was vulnerable and on the edge of sleep. Reminding me over and over I would never, ever find peace.

Gabriel.

Oh, sweets.

What have I done?

Like what you read? Find out more at
pattilarsen.com

Here's a look at the first chapter of
Book Eight of the Hayle Coven Destinies

BLOOD OF THE MAJI

ONE

He's falling again and I can't stop him, though I reach for him with the desperation of one who will not survive without him. The earth swallows his tall, beautiful form, devouring his strawberry blond waves, his hazel eyes flecked with green, until only one hand reaches upward for me, the earth eating him alive.

I scream his name, dive for him. It takes forever to hit the ground. It vibrates under me, the tiny seedling bursting from the dark loam that smells of fabric softener and spring. I have to leap away as the oak tree explodes from that tiny, green bit of life, erupting as though it had been waiting for this moment. It looms over me, vast and powerful, before it turns to steel.

My hands grasp for the metal tree, tears soaking the now hard ground, but he's gone and only this monolith of cold iron remains. But no, it's hot, heating up under my desperate grasp, burning me as I cry out and fall away.

Falling, into darkness.

And then I'm flying. The armor I wear is heavy on my shoulders but I barely feel it, welcome its presence. It's kept me alive so far, saves me as I take a hit to the chest from the distance while my mount wheels and dives to protect us from attack. The pressure of building power pushes against me, burning through the metal and scorching my skin, bruising my damaged body, crushing my chest so tight I have to fight for breath. I force my lungs to inflate out of sheer spite, scream a soundless yell of defiance, voice already parched and cracking, failing me.

But I will not fail.

My magic pulses, as weary as I am but refusing to quit while the massive wings of my drach friend sweep us forward, his power as unrelenting as my determination. We are together in the end, as we knew we would be, and I will not falter for he is with me.

We must reach them before it's too late.

The glowing, white sword of light hangs over my head, weightless, brilliant, shining a beacon in our fore, casting shadows over the sharp, violent spikes that adorn his once smooth, scaled shoulders. He is a weapon from the tip of his snout to the sharp edged blade of his tail, all of his creation now made for war. Designed by Creator to do what must be done.

We both are, now.

I clench tight the sword's hilt in my gauntlet, sweat running from my hot palm down inside my suit of living metal as my mount's massive head arches backward, fire spouting in a cascade of heat and ash blowing past my cheek. I inhale fire, choke on it, searing my insides. That hurt doesn't matter, won't stop me. Nothing will.

Another blow, this one to my head, carrying away the helm that guards my face. I shake off the strike, hair flying clear, ears ringing with the rush of impending death. I embrace it, suck it back like a draught of joy. We're almost there, the building juggernaut of destructive force between the armies hurtling toward each other narrowing by the instant.

We're almost too late. But Fate won't let us fall. Not now. Not ever.

We soar into the barest crack that remains, the bellow of my companion the trigger for the power bursting from us, the sword over my head erupting into a massive outward explosion of white sorcery that devours everything. I revel in it even as I accept my true destiny.

Doombringer. Light One. Wild Card of Creator.

Peace engulfs me while we die in the crushing press of the violent clash of their magic and ours.

I open my eyes in the darkness of my room, canopied bed quiet and empty save for me. I've curled into a ball, fetal position tight and rigid. It is impossible to unclasp, to release the tension. I need the support, holding myself together with this clasp of arms around knees, chest compressed to hold back my panting.

It is quiet in the house, oppressive and still. As lonely as my bed. Where is everyone? My magic reaches out, encounters nothing, not another soul. But that's not right, is it? The house should be full of people. Why then is it so empty?

But no, wait. There's another here. I feel myself unwind slowly, my hands unclenching from their grip on my arms to keep me in a ball, my legs relaxing, head turning toward the doorway of my room. And a faint light there.

He's smiling at me, his sweet face so kind and gentle. I smile back at my son only to find I can't, that I'm frozen, unable to move any more, locked in position as he crosses to me and sits on the side of the bed.

I can't even muster a meep of protest, a whimper of my need to sit up, to hold him. Why can't I move? Panic grips me while he bends close, his young face now aged, his father's face. I weep silently as my darling Gabriel presses his warm lips to my cheek.

"Mom," he says, voice ringing like a bell in my head. "Wake up."

ABOUT THE AUTHOR

Everything you need to know about me is in this one statement: I've wanted to be a writer since I was a little girl, and now I'm doing it. How cool is that, being able to follow your dream and make it reality? I've tried everything from university to college, graduating the second with a journalism diploma (I sucked at telling real stories), am part of an all-girl improv troupe (if you've never tried it, I highly recommend making things up as you go along as often as possible). I've even been in a Celtic girl band (some of our stuff is on YouTube!) and was an independent film maker. My life has been one creative thing after another—all leading me here, to writing books for a living.

Now with multiple series in happy publication, I live on beautiful and magical Prince Edward Island (I know you've heard of Anne of Green Gables) with my very patient husband and multitude of pets.

I love-love-love hearing from you! You can reach me (and I promise I'll message back) at patti@pattilarsen.com. And if you're eager for your next dose of Patti Larsen books (usually about one release a month) come join my mailing list! All the best up and coming, giveaways, contests and, of course, my observations on the world (aren't you just dying to know what I think about everything?) all in one place: http://smarturl.it/PattiLarsenEmail.

Last—but not least!—I hope you enjoyed what you read! Your happiness is my happiness. And I'd love to hear just what you thought. A review where you found this book would mean the world to me—reviews feed writers more than you will ever know. So, loved it (or not so much), **your honest review would make my day**. Thank you!